LYDDIE

"The courage of boys in the novels... dealt with often . . . but novels of this kind about girls are rare. *Lyddie* is outstanding because of the nature of its setting. . . . This is a rich story packed with a great variety of characters. . . . *Lyddie* is full of life, full of *lives*, full of reality." —*The New York Times Book Review*

"Readers will sympathize with Lyddie's hardships and admire her determination to create a better life for herself . . . Impeccably researched and expertly crafted, this book is sure to satisfy those interested in America's industrialization period." —*Publishers Weekly*

"[A] superb novel . . . Paterson has brought a troubling time and place vividly to life, but she has also given readers great hope in the spirited person of Lyddie Worthen." —*School Library Journal*, starred review

"The story and characterizations are Paterson at her best. Readers will carry the image of Lyddie with them for many years." —*Voice of Youth Advocates*

"A memorable portrait of an untutored but intelligent young woman making her way against fierce odds." —*Kirkus Reviews*, pointer review

KATHERINE PATERSON

Lyddie

PUFFIN BOOKS

PUFFIN BOOKS
Published by the Penguin Group
Penguin Books USA Inc., 375 Hudson Street, New York, New York 10014, U.S.A.
Penguin Books Ltd, 27 Wrights Lane, London W8 5TZ, England
Penguin Books Australia Ltd, Ringwood, Victoria, Australia
Penguin Books Canada Ltd, 10 Alcorn Avenue, Toronto, Ontario, Canada M4V 3B2
Penguin Books (N.Z.) Ltd, 182–190 Wairau Road, Auckland 10, New Zealand

Penguin Books Ltd, Registered Offices: Harmondsworth, Middlesex, England

First published in the United States of America by Lodestar Books,
an affiliate of Dutton Children's Books,
a division of Penguin Books USA Inc., 1991
Published in Puffin Books, 1992

1 3 5 7 9 10 8 6 4 2

LIBRARY OF CONGRESS CATALOGING-IN-PUBLICATION DATA
Paterson, Katherine.
    Lyddie / by Katherine Paterson.   p. cm.
    Summary: Impoverished Vermont farm girl Lyddie Worthen is
determined to gain her independence by becoming a factory worker in
Lowell, Massachusetts, in the 1840s.
    ISBN 0-14-034981-2
    [1. Self-reliance—Fiction. 2. Work—Fiction. 3. Factories—
Fiction. 4. Textile workers—Fiction. 5. Lowell (Mass.)—
Fiction.] I. Title.
[PZ7.P273Ly 1992]   [Fic]—dc20   92-20304

Printed in the United States of America
Set in Janson

for Stephen Pierce
our third son
and Friend in deed

Contents

1

The Bear

The bear had been their undoing, though at the time they had all laughed. No, Mama had never laughed, but Lyddie and Charles and the babies had laughed until their bellies ached. Lyddie still thought of them as the babies. She probably always would. Agnes had been four and Rachel six that November of 1843—the year of the bear.

It had been Charles's fault, if fault there was. He had fetched in wood from the shed and left the door ajar. But the door had not shut tight for some time, so perhaps he'd shut it as best he could. Who knows?

At any rate, Lyddie looked up from the pot of oatmeal she was stirring over the fire, and there in the doorway was a massive black head, the nose up and smelling, the tiny eyes bright with hungry anticipation.

"Don't nobody yell," she said softly. "Just back up slow and quiet to the ladder and climb up to the loft. Charlie, you get Agnes, and Mama, you take Rachel." She heard her mother whimper. "Shhh," she continued, her voice absolutely even. "It's all right long as nobody gets upset. Just take it nice and gentle, ey? I'm watching him all the way, and I'll yank the ladder up after me."

They obeyed her, even Mama, though Lyddie could hear her sucking in her breath. Behind Lyddie's back, the ladder creaked, as two by two, first Charles and Agnes, then Mama and Rachel, climbed up into the loft. Lyddie glared straight into the bear's eyes, daring him to step forward into the cabin. Then when the ladder was silent and she could hear the slight rustling above her as the family settled themselves on the straw mattresses, she backed up to the ladder and, never taking her eyes off the bear, inched her way up to the loft. At the top she almost fell backward onto the platform. Charles dragged her onto the mattress beside her mother.

The racket released the bear from the charm Lyddie seemed to have placed on him. He banged the door aside and rushed in toward the ladder, but Charles snatched it. The bottom rungs swung out, hitting the beast in the nose. The blow startled him momentarily, giving Lyddie a chance to help Charles haul the ladder up onto the platform and out of reach. The old bear roared in frustration and waved at the empty air with his huge paws, then reared up on his hind legs. He was so tall that his nose nearly touched the edge of the loft. The little girls cried out. Their mother screamed, "Oh Lord, deliver us!"

"Hush," Lyddie commanded. "You'll just make him madder." The cries were swallowed up in anxious gasps of breath. Charles's arms went around the little ones, and Lyddie put a firm grip on her mother's shoulder. It was trembling, so Lyddie relaxed her fingers and began to stroke. "It's all right," she murmured. "He can't reach us."

But could he climb the supports? It didn't seem likely. Could he, in his frustration, take a mighty leap and . . . No, she tried to breathe deeply and evenly and keep her eyes fixed on those of the beast. He fell to all fours and, tossing his head, broke off from her gaze as though embarrassed. He began to explore the cabin. He was hungry, obviously, and looking for the source of the smell that had drawn him in. He knocked over the churning jug and licked tentatively at the blade, but Lyddie had cleaned it too well after churning that morning and the critter soon gave up trying to find nourishment in the wood.

Before he found the great pot of oatmeal in the kettle over the fire, he had turned over the table and the benches and upended the spinning wheel. Lyddie held her breath, praying that he wouldn't break anything. Charles and she would try to mend, but he was only ten and she thirteen. They hadn't their father's skill or experience. *Don't break nothing*, she begged silently. They couldn't afford to replace any of the household goods.

Next the beast knocked over a jar of apple butter, but the skin lid was tied on tightly, and, flail away at it as he might with his awkward paw, he could not dislodge it. He smacked it across the floor where it hit the overturned bench, but, thank the Lord, the heavy pottery did not shatter.

At last he came to the oatmeal, bubbling—by the smell of it, scorching—over the fire. He thrust his head deep into the kettle and howled with pain as his nose met the boiling porridge. He threw back his head, but in doing so jerked the kettle off the hook, and when he turned, he was wearing it over his head like a black pumpkin. The bear was too stunned, it seemed, simply to lower his neck and let the kettle fall off. He danced about the room in pain on four, then two legs, the kettle covering his head, the boiling oatmeal raining down his thick neck and coat.

He knocked about, searching for the way out, but when he found the open door, managed to push it shut. Battering the door with his kettle-covered head, he tore it off its leather hinges and loped out into the dark. For a long time they could hear him crashing through the bush until, at last, the November night gathered about them once more with its accustomed quiet.

Then they began to laugh. Rachel first, throwing back her dark curls and showing the spaces where her pretty little teeth had been only last summer. Then Agnes joined in with her shrill four-year-old shout, and next Charles's not yet manly giggle.

"Whew," Lyddie said. "Lucky I'm so ugly. A pretty girl couldn't a scared that old rascal!"

"You ain't ugly!" Rachel cried. But they laughed louder than ever, Lyddie the loudest of all, until the tears of laughter and relief ran down her thin cheeks, and her belly cramped and doubled over. When had she laughed so much? She could not remember.

Her mother's shoulders were shaking, but Lyddie couldn't see her face. Mama must be laughing too. Lyddie dared to hope that her mother might laugh. Oh, there was the door to mend and the mess to be cleaned up, and the wasted porridge. But tomorrow she and Charles would find the kettle. The bear couldn't have taken it far and he was sure to have left more than an adequate trail with all that crashing through the underbrush. Let her be laughing, she prayed.

"Mama," she whispered, leaning her mouth close to her mother's ear. "You all right, ey?"

Her mother whirled toward her. "It's the sign," she said.

"What sign, Mama?" Lyddie asked, though she did not want an answer.

"Clarissa said when the end drew near, the devil would walk the earth."

"That weren't no devil, Mama," Charles said. "It were only a black bear."

" 'Your adversary the devil prowls around like a roaring lion, seeking whom he may devour.' "

"Aunt Clarissa don't know, Mama," Lyddie said as firmly as she could, though a shudder went through her body.

"It were only a black bear." Rachel's anxious little voice echoed her brother's, and then, "Weren't it, Lyddie? Weren't it a bear?"

4

Lyddie nodded, so as not to seem to be contradicting their mother out loud.

"Tomorrow we're going to Poultney," their mother said. "I aim to be with the faithful when the end comes."

"I don't want to be with the fate full," Rachel said. "I want to be with Lyddie."

"Lyddie will come too," their mother said.

"But how will Papa find us if we've left home?" Charles asked.

"Your father went out searching for vain riches. He ain't never coming back."

"He will! He will!" Rachel cried. "He promised." Though how could she remember? She'd been barely three when he'd left.

It was hard for the babies to go to sleep. Their stomachs were empty since the porridge had been ruined, and Mama would not hear of fixing more. Charles helped Lyddie clean the cabin. They propped up the door and put the chest against it to keep it in place until they could fix it in the morning. Then he climbed up the ladder to bed.

Lyddie stayed below. The fire must be banked for the night. She knelt down on the hearth. Behind her left shoulder sat Mama in the one chair, a rocker she had brought from Poultney when she came as a bride. Lyddie stole a glance at her. She was rocking like one dazed, staring unblinking into the fire.

The truth be told, Mama had gone somewhat queer in the head after their father had left. Lyddie had to acknowledge it. Not so strange as her sister, Clarissa, and her end-of-the-world-shouting husband, Judah—surely not. But now the bear seemed to have pushed her too far. "Don't let's go, Mama," Lyddie pleaded softly. "Please, Mama." But her mama only stared at the fireplace, rocking slowly back and forth, her eyes blank and still as though her spirit had gone away and left the body there rocking on and on.

It was useless to argue, and Lyddie gave up, hoping that the mood would pass, like her mother's times of craziness always had. But the next morning her mother had not forgotten her determination. "If it ain't Clarissa's, it will soon be the poor farm," she said.

The only charity Lyddie dreaded more than Aunt Clarissa's was that of the township's poor farm. It was to escape that specter that their father had headed West.

"I can't stop you to go," Lyddie said, "but I can't go with you. I can't leave the farm." When her mother opened her mouth to argue, Lyddie went on. "The sow won't fetch enough to provide coach fare for the lot of us."

She sent Charles along to make sure her mother and the babies arrived safely at Uncle Judah's farm. Charlie was a funny sight, hardly higher than a currant bush, but drawn up like a man in his worn boots and his father's old woolen shirt with the sleeves rolled. He loaded up the barrow; they'd sold the horse cart for seeds last year. "It's only ten miles to Cutler's, where the coach stops. The little ones can ride when they get too tired," he said. He put in their mother's old skin trunk, which had carried her meager trousseau to this mountain and most of the food she'd managed to preserve before she gave up trying. Between them, he and Lyddie wrestled the old sow to the ground and tied her, squealing, to a shaft of the barrow.

"You want I should go with you as far as the village?" she asked him. But they agreed it would be better for her to tend the cow and horse and protect the house from the wild critters.

"You watch out for yourself," he said anxiously.

"I'll do fine," she said. "Now remember, you got to get enough for the pig to pay coach fare for everyone."

"And for me to come back again," he said, as a promise that she would not be left alone on the mountain farm. He glanced about to make sure his mother wasn't in hearing distance. "You mustn't be afraid to go down and ask the Quaker Stevens for help, Lyddie. They mean to be good neighbors to us, no matter what Mama says."

"Well, I'll see how it goes, ey?" she said, tossing her thin plaits behind her shoulders. He should know she was not going to be beholden to the neighbors for anything so trivial as her own comfort. Their mother didn't approve of heathens or abolitionists, and since she considered their Quaker neighbors a bit of both, she forbade the children to have anything to do with the Stevenses. "Ain't no Worthen gonna have truck with the devil," she said. Early last summer, when Mama was having one of her spells and not paying much attention, Charlie had again sneaked the cow down the mountain to the Stevenses' place. As long as Lyddie could remember, long before their father had left, they had made use of the Stevenses' bull. If their mother ever wondered about those calves that were born like miracles every spring, she never mentioned it. She knew as well as Lyddie and Charles that they could never have managed without the cash money those calves brought in.

Lyddie didn't care one way or the other about the neighbors' radical ideas and peculiar ways, she minded mightily being beholden. It couldn't be helped. The use of a bull was a necessity she couldn't manage on her own, but she would starve to death rather than go begging before this year's calf was safely born and it was time to mate the cow once more.

She needn't have worried. Charlie came back in about two weeks, and together they made it through the winter. They shot rabbits and peeled bark for soup to eke out their scarce provisions. They ran out of flour for bread, so the churn stood idle, but "I never craved churning," said Lyddie.

When the time for the calving drew near, they reluctantly let the cow go dry. They had no need for butter without any bread, but they'd miss the milk and cheese sorely. Nonetheless, they were farmers enough to do what was best for their only cow.

The calf was born to great rejoicing and a new abundance of milk and cream. Lyddie and Charles felt rich as townsfolk. A sweet little heifer she was, arriving on the first warm day of March, the same day that they bored holes in the sugar maples and inserted the spills that they had made to catch the sap flow. They were able to make enough syrup and sugar for themselves. Hardly enough for a cash crop, but they were learning, and in another year, after another harvest, they would be experienced old farmers and sugarers, they told each other.

Years later she would remember that morning. The late May sky was brilliant dare-you-to-wink blue, and the cheek of the hillside wore a three-day growth of green. High in one of the apple trees a bluebird warbled his full spring song, *chera, weera, wee-it, cheerily-cheerily*. Lyddie's own spirit rose in reply. Her rough hands were stretched to grasp the satin-smooth wooden shafts of the old plow. With Charles at the horse's head, they urged and pushed the heavy metal blade through the rocky earth. The plow cast up the clean, damp smell of new turned soil. *Cheerily-cheerily*.

Then into that perfect spring morning a horse and rider had come round the narrow curve of the road, slowly, the horse gingerly picking its way across the deep, dried ruts of mud left from the thaws of April and early May.

"Charlie," she said quietly, hardly daring to move, because for a moment she hoped it might be Papa, but only for a moment. It was plainly a woman riding sidesaddle, and not their mother, either. She never rode since she fell years ago and miscarried the baby that would have come between Lyddie and Charles.

"Charlie," Lyddie repeated. "Someone's coming."

Mrs. Peck, for she was the rider, had brought a letter from

the general store in the village. "I thought you might be wanting this," she said. Lyddie fetched the coins for the postage from their almost empty cash box. The shopkeeper's wife waited a bit, hoping, perhaps, that Lyddie would read the letter aloud, but she didn't. Lyddie was not much of a reader, so it was later, the short wisps of hair around her face plastered with sweat, that she held the letter close to the fire and managed to make out the words in her mother's cramped and painfully childish hand.

Dear Lyddie,
 The world hav not come to the end yit. But we can stil hop. Meentime I hav hire you out to M. Cutler at the tavern and fer yr. brother to Bakers mill. The paschur, feelds and sugar bush is lent to M. Wescott to repay dets. Also cow and horse. Lv. at wuns you git this.
Yr. loving mother,
Mattie M. Worthen

Lyddie burst into tears. "I'm sorry, Charlie," she said to her brother's amazed and anxious face. "I never expected this. We were doing so good, ey? You and me."

He took a deep breath, reached into his pocket, and handed her a ragged kerchief.

"It's all right, Lyddie," he said. "It's all right." When she kept her tear-streaked face buried in his kerchief, he gave one of her braids a tweak. "The world have not come to the end yit, ey?" He took the letter from her lap, and when she wiped her face and tried to smile, he grinned anxiously and pointed to their mother's primitive spelling. "See, we can stil hop."

Lyddie laughed uncertainly. Her spelling was no better than their mother's, so she did not really see the joke at first. But Charlie laughed, and so she began to laugh, though it was the kind of laughter that caught like briars in her chest and felt very much like pain.

2
Kindly Friends

"She didn't say nothing about the calf," Lyddie said suddenly in the midst of their sorrowful packing up.

"She got no cause to," Charles said. "We never tell her about it."

"You know, Charlie, that calf is rightfully ours."

He looked at her, his honest head cocked, his eyes dubious.

"No, truly. We was the ones asked Quaker Stevens to lend us use of his bull. Mama didn't have nothing to do with it."

"But if they's debts . . ."

"She's letting out the fields and the horse and cow. She's sending you to be a miller's boy and me to housemaid. She's got us body and soul. We got no call to give her the calf." She set one hand on her waist and straightened her aching back.

"What do you aim to do with it?"

"Hush. I'm studying on it." Obediently, he quieted and stared in the same direction at the spindly maples that made up their stand of sugar bush.

"It's a nice fat heifer," she said. "We kept it so long on its mother's milk. We'll get a good price for it."

"We'd be bound to give the money to her."

"No." Her voice was sharper than she meant, ground as it was on three years of unspoken anger. "We always done that and look where it's got us. No," she said again, this time softly. "The money don't go there. She'll give it away to Uncle Judah, who'll give it to that preacher who says you don't need nothing 'cause the world is going to end." She turned to her brother. "Charlie, you and me can't think about that. We got to think about keeping this farm for when Papa comes back. We should take that money and bury it someplace, so when we get free we can come back here and have a little seed cash to start over with."

"Maybe she'll sell the farm."

"She can't. Not so long as Papa's alive."

"But maybe . . ."

"We don't know that, now do we? We got to believe he's coming back—or he's sending for us."

"I hope he don't send for us."

"We'll persuade him to stay," she said. She wanted for a minute to put her arm around his thin shoulders, but she held back. She didn't want him to think that she considered him less than the man he had so bravely sought to be. "We're a good team, ey, Charlie?"

"Ox or mule?" he asked, grinning.

"A little of both, I reckon."

They cleaned the cabin and swept out the splintery plank floor. They knew it was a rough and homely place compared to the farmhouses along the road and the ample mansions around the village green. But their father, the seventh son of a poor Connecticut Valley farmer, had bought the land and built the cabin with his own hands before their birth, promising every year to sell enough maple sugar, or oats, or potash to build a larger, proper house with a real barn attached instead of a shed which must be found through rain or blizzard. His sugar bush was scraggly and his oat crop barely enough to feed his growing family. There were stumps to burn aplenty as he cleared the land, but suddenly there was no need for potash in England and hardly any demand in Vermont. He borrowed heavily to buy himself three sheep, and the bottom dropped out of the wool market the very year he had had enough wool to think of it as a cash crop. He was an unlucky man. Even his children sensed that, but he loved them and worked hard for them, and they loved him fiercely in return.

Pulling shut the door, which, despite all Charles's efforts, still did not close quite flush, they remembered the bear and wondered how they could keep the wild creatures from destroying the cabin in their absence. Finally, Charles suggested that they take all the wood left in the woodpile and stack it in front of the door. It took them close to an hour to accomplish the move, but, sweating and breathing hard, they admired their fortress effect.

That made it a little easier for them to go. Charlie rode bareback astride the plow horse, his brown heels dug into the horse's wide flanks. Lyddie, leading the cow, followed close by. She carried a gunnysack, which held her other dress and night shift. Her outgrown boots were joined by the laces and slung over her shoulder. The long walk would be more easily done with her feet free and bare. There was no need to tie the calf. It danced around its mother's backside, bleating constantly for her to stand still long enough for a meal.

It was the end of May. The mud was drying in the deeply rutted roadway, but Lyddie did not watch her feet. Birds were playing in and out of the tall trees on either side of the road, calling and singing in the pale lacy greens and rusts of the new growth and the deep green of the pines and firs. Here and there wildflowers dared to dance in full summer dress, forgetting that any night might bring a killing frost.

Lyddie breathed in the sweet air. "It's spring," she said. Charles nodded.

"Do you mind too much going to the mill?" she asked.

He shrugged. "I don't rightly know. Don't seem too bad. Dusty, I reckon. And not much time to be lazy, ey?"

She laughed. "You wouldn't know how to be lazy, Charlie."

He smiled at the compliment. "I'd rather be home."

She sighed. "We'll be back, Charlie, I promise." They were both quiet a moment remembering their father saying almost the same words. "Truly," she added. "I'm sure of it."

He smiled. "Sure," he said.

They were in sight now of Quaker Stevens's farm. They could see him, his broad-brimmed straight black hat surrounded by the black hats of his three grown sons. They had the oxen yoked to a sled, which was already half loaded with stones, and were digging away at more stones buried in a newly cleared field.

Their farmhouse, close to the road, had been added onto over the years. The outlines of the first saltbox could be made out on the northern end, which melted on the backside into a larger frame Cape Cod, then an ell that served as shed, storage, privy, and corridor to two barns, the larger one growing out of the smaller. They were rich for all their Quaker adherence to the simple life.

Envy crept up like a noxious vine. Lyddie snapped it off, but the roots were deep and beyond her reach.

Before they called out, the farmer had seen them. He waved, took off his hat to wipe his head and face on the sleeve of his homespun shirt, replaced his hat, and made his way across the field to the road.

"I see my bull served thee well," he said, smiling. His face was broad and red, his hair curly and gray about his ears. Great caterpillar eyebrows crowned his kindly eyes.

"We come to thank you," Lyddie began, thinking fast, wanting to be fair and honest but at the same time wanting a large price for the calf that she knew in her heart was partly his.

"Thee brought these beasts five miles down the road for that?" he asked, his woolly eyebrows high up on his forehead.

Lyddie blushed. "The truth is, we're taking the horse and cow to Mr. Westcott—in payment of debt, and we're obliged to sell off this pretty calf straight away. Our mother's put us out to work."

"Thee's leaving thy land?"

"It's let as well," she said, allowing just a tiny hint of sadness to creep into her voice. "Charles here and I was waiting for our father to come back from the West, but . . ."

"Thee's been alone all winter, just thee two children?"

She could feel Charles stiffen beside her. "We managed fine," she said.

He took off his hat again and wiped his face and neck. "I should have come to call on my neighbors," he said quietly.

She sensed a weakness. "You wouldn't be interested . . . no, surely not. You got a mighty herd already."

"I'll give thee twenty dollars for the calf," he said quickly. "No, twenty-five. I know the sire and he's of a good line." He smiled.

Lyddie pretended to think. "Seems mighty high," she said.

"She's half yours by rights," Charles blurted out before Lyddie could elbow him quiet. His honesty would be her death yet.

But the kind man persisted. "It's a fair price for a nice fat little heifer. Thee's kept her well."

He invited them in to complete their business transaction and, before they were done, they found themselves eating a hearty noon dinner with the family. The room they sat down in was larger than the whole cabin with the shed thrown in. It was kitchen and parlor with a corner for spinning and weaving. The Quakers were rich enough to own their own loom. The meal spread out on the long oak table looked like a king's feast to children who, until the cow freshened, had lived mostly on rabbit and bark soup, and the last of the moldy potatoes from the year before.

The Quaker's wife was as large and red-faced as her husband, and equally kind. She urged them to eat, for they still had a long walk ahead of them. This reminded Quaker Stevens that he needed nails. One of the boys could take them to the mill and then on to the village, he said. The cow and horse must be tethered to the back of the wagon, so it would be nearly as slow as walking until they got to Westcott's, but, if they'd care for the ride . . .

The sons had removed their hats for the meal. They looked much younger and less stern than she remembered them. The youngest, Luke, she had seen more often, back in the days when she had gone to school. He had been one of the enormous boys who sat in the back of the schoolroom—sixteen or so when she was a tiny one in the front row. She hadn't gone to school at all since her father left. She hadn't dared to leave the babies alone with their mother. Charles had gone for most of the four-month term up until this past winter—until it had seemed too hard. She hoped the miller would let him do some schooling. He had a good mind, not so stubborn against learning as hers seemed to be.

Luke Stevens tied the horse and cow to the back of the wagon and then came around to give Lyddie a hand up, but she pretended not to see. She couldn't have the man thinking she was a child or a helpless female. She jumped up the high step into the wagon and then realized she'd be squeezed between Luke and Charles on the narrow seat. She sat as tightly into herself as she could. She wasn't used to brushing bodies with near strangers. They hardly touched one another in the family. It made her feel small and tongue-tied to be so close to this great hulk of a man.

He wasn't much of a talker either. He leaned forward from time to time and talked around her to Charles. He asked if

Charlie knew much about the mill where he'd be working. Charles's sweet, high-pitched boyish tones made him seem heartbreakingly young against the deep male voice of his questioner. It was so unfair. This man had both father and mother and older brothers to live with and to care for him, while little Charlie must make his way in the world alone. She felt around the bottom of the gunnysack until her fingers found the lump of coinage. She pinched the money hard to remind herself not to cry.

"Then the farm will just lie fallow?" Luke was asking Charles.

"No, it's let—the fields and pasture and sugar bush for the debt. The house and shed we'll just leave be. I hope the snow don't do in the roofs." Charles's anxious concern was almost too much for Lyddie to bear.

"Oh, they'll be all right. And we'll be back in a couple of years."

"I could stop by. Would thee like me to stop by? Shovel the snow off the roof if need be?"

"No need . . ." she started, but Charles was already thanking him for his kindness.

"I'd be obliged," he said. "It would take the worry off. Lyddie and me aim to keep it standing against Papa's return. Don't make it trouble for yourself, though."

"It'd be no trouble," Luke said kindly.

"Ain't nobody to pack down the track come snow."

He ignored her grumpy tone, smiling at her. "I can snowshoe it. Nothing better than a good hike on my own. That house gets mighty crowded come winter." The way he spoke made Lyddie feel that she was the child and Charles the responsible one.

The horse and cow were safely delivered to Mr. Westcott. His farm lay in the river plain and was already alive with shoots of new corn. Lyddie watched Mr. Westcott lead their old cow and horse away. Next to Westcott's sleek stock, they'd look like hungry sparrows pecking in a hen yard.

At a livelier clip they took the river road toward Baker's Mill. "I can walk from here easy," Charles protested, but Luke shook him off. "Faster I get home, sooner I'm hauling rocks," he said, laughing.

She didn't want Luke Stevens watching while she bid Charles good-bye, but again maybe it was better. She might weaken if they were alone, and that would never do.

"I'll only be in the village," she said. "Maybe you can drop up."

Charles put his little hand on her arm. "You mustn't worry, ey Lyddie," he said. "You'll be all right."

She nearly laughed. He was trying to comfort her. Or maybe she nearly cried. She watched the gaping mouth of the mill swallow up his small form. He turned in the immense doorway—it was large enough to drive a high wagon through—and waved. "Let's be going," she said. "It's late."

Luke nodded his head with a dip of his funny black hat. "This here is Cutler's Tavern," he said. They hadn't spoken since they left the mill. "Shall I come to the door with thee?" The wagon had stopped before a low stone wall, hung with a rail gate.

She was horrified. "No, no need," she said. "They might not understand me riding up with a . . ." She scrambled to the ground.

He grinned. "I hope to see thee before too much time is up," he said. "Meantime, I'll see to thy house." He leaned over the seat. "I'll give a look in on thy Charlie, too," he said. "He's a good boy."

She didn't know whether to be pleased or annoyed, but he clicked his tongue and the wagon pulled away, leaving her alone in her new life.

3

Cutler's Tavern

Lyddie stood outside the gate, waiting until Luke and his wagon disappeared around the curve of the road. Then she watched a pair of swallows dive and soar around the huge chimney in the center of the main house. The tavern was larger than the Stevenses' farmhouse. Addition after addition, porch, shed, and a couple of barns, the end one at least four stories high. The whole complex, recently painted with a mix of red ochre and buttermilk, stood against the sky like a row of giant beets popped clear of the earth.

The pastures, a lush new green, were dotted with merino sheep and fat milk cows. There was a huge sugar maple in front of what must be the parlor door, and another at the porch, which, from the presence of churns and cooling pans, must lead into the kitchen.

Once I walk in that gate, I ain't free anymore, she thought. No matter how handsome the house, once I enter I'm a servant girl—no more than a black slave. She had been queen of the cabin and the straggly fields and sugar bush up there on the hill. But now someone else would call the tune. How could her mother have done such a thing? She was sure her father would be horrified—she and Charlie drudges on someone else's place. It didn't matter that plenty of poor people put out their children for hire to save having to feed them. She and Charlie could have fed themselves—just one good harvest—one good sugaring—that was all they needed. And they could have stayed together.

She was startled out of her dreaming by a hideous roar, and before she could figure out what animal could have made such a noise, a stagecoach appeared, drawn by two spans of sweating Morgan horses, shaking their great heads, showing their fierce teeth, saliva foaming on their iron bits. The coach had rounded the curve, its horn bellowing.

The driver was yelling as well, and then, just in time, she realized that he was yelling at her. She jumped hard against the wall. He was still yelling back at her as he pulled up the reins, the coach itself now on the very spot where she had been standing seconds before.

Should she apologize? No, he wasn't paying her any attention now. He was turning the team over to a boy who had run out of the shed. A woman was hurrying out of the kitchen door to welcome the passengers, who were climbing stiffly from the coach. Lyddie stared. They were very grand looking. One of the gentlemen, a man in a beaver hat and frilled shirt, turned to hand a woman down the coach step. The lady's face was hidden by a fancy straw bonnet, the brim decorated with roses that matched her gown. Was it silk? Lyddie couldn't be sure, never having seen a real silk dress before, but it was smooth and pink like a baby's cheek. Around her shoulders the lady wore a shawl woven in a deeper shade of pink. Lyddie marveled that the woman would wear something so delicate for a ride to the northland in a dusty coach.

Safely on the ground, the woman lifted her head and looked about her. Her face was thin and white, her features elegant. She caught Lyddie's eyes and smiled. It was a very nice smile, not at all haughty. Lyddie realized that she had been staring. She closed her mouth and quickly looked away.

Then the encounter was over, for the stout woman who had come out of the kitchen door was hustling the lady, her escort, and two other passengers through the low gate and around to the main door at the north end of the tavern.

Suddenly she saw Lyddie. She came over to the wall and whispered hoarsely across it to her. "What are you doing here?" She was looking Lyddie up and down as she asked, as though Lyddie were a stray dog who had wandered too close to her house.

Lyddie was aware, as she might not have been minutes before, that she had no bonnet and that her hair and braids were dusty from the road. She crossed her arms, trying to cover her worn brown homespun with the gunnysack. The dress was tight across her newly budding chest, and it hung unevenly to just above her ankles in a ragged hem. Her brown feet were bare, her outgrown boots still slung over her shoulder. She should have remembered to put them on before she got off Luke's wagon.

Self-consciously, she raised her sleeve and wiped her nose and mouth under the woman's unforgiving stare. "Go along," the woman was saying. "This is a respectable tavern, not the township poor farm."

Lyddie could feel the rage oozing up like sap on a March morning. She cleared her throat and stood up straight. "I'm Lydia Worthen," she said. "I got a letter from my mother . . ."

The woman looked horrified. "You're the new girl?"

"I reckon I am," Lyddie said, clutching her gunnysack more tightly.

"Well, I've no time to bother with you now," the woman said. "Go into the kitchen and ask Triphena to tell you where you can wash. We keep a clean place here."

Lyddie bit her lip to keep from answering back. She looked straight into the woman's face until the woman blinked and turned, running a little to catch up with the guests who were waiting for her at the main door.

The cook was as busy as the mistress and not eager to involve herself with a dirty new servant just when she was putting the meal on the table. "Sit over there." Triphena shook her head at a low stool near the huge fireplace. Lyddie would rather have stood after the long, bumpy ride in the Stevenses' wagon, but she chose not to cause a problem with the cook as well as with the mistress in the first ten minutes of her employment.

The kitchen was three times the size of the whole Worthen cabin. Its center was the huge fireplace. Lyddie could have stretched out full length in front of it and her head and toes would have remained on the hearth with room to spare.

Built into the right side of the brick chimney was a huge beehive-shaped oven, and the smell of fresh-baked loaves made Lyddie forget the generous dinner she'd shared noontime. The trouble with eating good, she thought later, is you get too used to it. You think you ought to have it regular, not just for a treat.

Over the fire hung a kettle so large that both the babies could have bathed in it together. It was bubbling with a meat stew chock-full of carrots and onions and beans and potatoes in a thick brown broth. There were chickens turning on a spit, which seemed to be magically going round and round on its own. But as Lyddie's eyes followed a leather strap upward, she saw, above the fireplace, the mechanism from which hung a huge metal pendulum. She wished her father could see it. He could make one perhaps from wood and then no one would have to tediously turn the spit by hand. But perhaps it was something you'd have to order from the blacksmith—in which case it was likely to be so dear that only the rich could afford one. She couldn't remember seeing one at the Stevenses', and they were rich enough to own their own loom.

"Move," the cook said. The large woman was beginning to take the food from the fire. She gave Lyddie a quick glance. "Lucky you're so plain. Guests couldn't leave the last girl be." She was ladling stew into a large serving basin. "Won't have no trouble with you, will we?"

Lyddie picked up the stool and moved to a corner of the room. She knew she was no beauty, never had been, but she was a fierce worker. She'd prove that to the woman. Should she offer to help now? But the cook was too busy moving the food from the fire to the long wooden table in the center of the room to pay her any mind. Lyddie scrunched her body into itself and tucked her bare feet under the low stool, fearful of seeming in the way. Would all the guests come in here to eat? And if so, where should she hide?

As if to answer her question, the mistress pushed through the door with a boy behind her. "Hurry," she said. She supervised while the last of the food was transferred from the iron kettles into great china basins, which the cook and the boy carried from the kitchen to some other part of the house. The mistress mumbled and grumped orders, and in between complained of the guest who made herself out to be a lady when she was nothing but a factory girl putting on fancy airs.

If the mistress saw Lyddie sitting in the corner, she never let on. Lyddie was glad to be ignored. She needed time and a chance to wash and change her dusty clothes. If only she hadn't worn her better homespun to travel in. The one in the gunnysack was even tighter and more ragged. She hadn't had a new dress since they sold the sheep four years ago. Since then, her body had begun to make those strange changes to womanhood that exasperated her. Why couldn't she be as thin and straight as a boy? Why couldn't she have been a boy? Perhaps, then, her father would not have had to leave. With an older son to help, maybe he could have made a living for them on the hill farm.

But, hard as she wished, hard as she tried, she was only a girl. She was, as girls go, scrawny and muscular, yet her boyish frame had in the last year betrayed her. Her breasts were small and her hips only slightly curved, but she couldn't help resenting these visible signs that she was doomed to be female.

Even the last year before Papa left, he had begun sending her in to help her mother. "She never really got over the baby's birth," he'd say. But once there was no more wool to spin, she felt as though her presence in the house just made her mother try less. One by one, the household tasks had been turned over to Lyddie—cooking and churning and cleaning and caring for the babies. For a while her mother spun the flax. They had no loom and paid the village weaver in spun flax for cloth. Her father had left them in a new shirt her mother had made. But that was the last garment her mother sewed. Lyddie tried to keep up the spinning, but when she had to take her father's place outdoors, she was too exhausted to try to spin and sew in the dim candlelight.

Last winter she sewed one shirt. She had made it for Charlie because he, too, was outgrowing his clothes, and the old wool shirt their father had left behind hung on him like a nightdress.

As it turned out, Mistress Cutler provided her with a store-bought calico gown. It was softer than her rough brown home-spun and fit her much better, but somehow it suited her less. How could she enjoy the garment of her servitude? She was fit with new boots as well. They pinched her feet and made her long to go barefoot, but she wore them, if not meekly, at least with determined obedience. After a few weeks and many blisters, they softened a little, and she was able to forget them for an hour or so at a time.

The people at Cutler's were not so easy to forget. The mistress was large in body and seemed to be everywhere on watch. How could a woman so obviously rich in this world's goods be so mean in the use of them? Her eyes were narrow and close and always on the sharp for the least bit of spilt flour or the odd crumb on the lip.

Not that Lyddie would stoop to steal a bite of bread. But the boy, Willie Hyde, was given to snatching the last of the loaf as he carried the breadbasket from the table to the kitchen. He was a year or so older than Charles and growing like red birch, and to hear the mistress carry on, about as useless. He was sent to shed or barn or field whenever he was not needed in the tavern itself. Lyddie would not have said so, but she envied him the chance to be outdoors and out of boots so often.

Mistress Cutler watched Lyddie like a barn cat on a sparrow, but Lyddie was determined not to give her cause for complaint. She had worked hard since she could remember. But now she worked even harder, for who was there to share a moment's leisure with? Who would listen with her to a bird call, stare at the sunset, or watch a calf stumble on its long, funny legs toward its mother? Missing Charlie was like wearing a stone around her neck.

She slept under the eaves in a windowless passage, which was hot and airless even in late spring. She was ordered to bed late and obliged to rise early, for the mistress was determined that no paying guest in the windowed rooms across the narrow passageway should know that they shared the floor with the kitchen girl.

She spoke rarely, but she listened intently, storing up stories for Charlie. She didn't consider writing him. She was ashamed to have Charlie see her poor penmanship and crude spelling and, besides, there was no money for paper or postage—nothing except the calf money, and she would not spent a half penny of that. Indeed, at night when she was too tired or too hot to sleep, she would take the gunnysack out from under her straw mattress and count the money in the darkness. It's like little Agnes sucking her thumb, she scolded herself, but she didn't stop. It was the only comfort she had that summer.

It was nearly September when she saw the pink silk lady again. She had come this time on the coach from Burlington, and was headed, Lyddie overheard her say at supper, for Lowell, Massachusetts. When another traveler asked her business in Lowell, she smiled and said, "Why I work in the Hamilton Mill there. Yes," she added, answering her questioner's stare, "I'm one of those *factory girls*."

The man murmured something and turned his face toward his bowl of stew.

The lady watched him, still smiling, and then, catching Lyddie's eye, smiled even more broadly, as though to imply that Lyddie was a comrade in some peculiar way.

Indeed, when the men had left the dining room to go into the taproom, she stayed behind, reading a book she had taken from a small silk purse that matched her lovely dress.

"I've seen you before, haven't I?"

Lyddie looked around to see to whom the lady was speaking, then realized the room was empty except for the two of them.

"In late May, when I was headed home to the farm for the summer."

Lyddie cleared her throat. She had lost the habit of conversation. She nodded.

"You're not one of the family here."

Lyddie shook her head.

"You're a good worker. I can see that."

Lyddie nodded again to acknowledge the compliment and turned again to loading the dirty dishes on her tray.

"You'd do well in the mill, you know. You'd clear at least two dollars a week. And"—she paused—"you'd be independent."

She was lying, Lyddie was sure of it. No girl could make that much money in a week's time.

"It's hard work, but maybe easier than what you do here, and you'd have some time to yourself, to study or just rest."

"My mother's promised me here," Lyddie said quickly because the door from the kitchen was moving and suddenly Mistress Cutler was in the dining room. The woman looked from the lady to Lyddie, opening her mouth to speak, but Lyddie didn't wait. She hurried past her into the kitchen.

That night, again she counted the calf money. The lady had been lying, of course. But still, how had a farmer's daughter bought a silk dress?

4

Frog in a Butter Churn

When Lyddie first came to the tavern, Willie built up the morning fire. But he overslept often and several times the fire went out and someone had to be sent to the neighbor's for live coals. The mistress was too mean to invest in a tinderbox, but she was mortified to be thought a careless housewife who let her kitchen fire die, so she put Lyddie in charge of it.

The first few nights Lyddie was fearful that she would not wake up early enough in her windowless room and slept on the hearth all night, so as to be sure to be the first up in the morning.

Triphena came in one morning and found her there, but instead of scolding, took pity. A sort of friendship began that morning. The cook was past her middle years and homely. She had never married, preferring, as she said, "not to be a slave to any man." She was large and vigorous, impatient with Willie, who had to be told things more than once, but, as the days wore on, won over by Lyddie's hard work and quiet ways.

One morning while Lyddie was churning, just as the cream was breaking into curdles, the cook told Lyddie about the two frogs who fell into the pail of milk. "One drowned right off," she said, nodding her head in the direction of the door, which had just slammed shut behind Willie's back. "But the other kicked and kicked, and in the morning they found him there, floating on a big pat of butter."

Lyddie smiled despite herself.

"Ehyeh," Triphena continued. "Some folks are natural born kickers. They can always find a way to turn disaster into butter."

We can stil hop. Lyddie nearly laughed out loud.

Triphena cocked her head in question, but Lyddie only smiled and shook her head. She couldn't share Charlie's joke with someone else.

Autumn came all too quickly. The days grew suddenly short. And never, though she dreamed and plotted as she scrubbed the iron kettles and churned the butter and bellowed up the fire, never a chance to take the calf money home.

There was no word from Charlie. Not that she truly expected a letter—they had neither money for stationery and postage nor the time or energy for composition. She tried to keep him in her mind—to picture, as she lay upon her own cot, how he was growing and what he was doing. She rarely thought of Rachel and Agnes or their mother. The three of them seemed to belong to another, sadder life. The possibility of their father's return slipped into a back corner of her mind. She wondered once if he were dead, and that was why she seldom thought of him now. There was no pain in the thought, only a kind of numb curiosity.

She and Charlie had left their mother's note and notes of their own to Papa on the table in the cabin, weighted down by the heavy iron candlestick, so, in case he returned, he would know where they were. But the old vision of him coming up the narrow track had faded like a worn-out garment. When she realized that the dream she'd clutched for three years had slipped from her grasp, she wondered if she should feel bad that she had lost it. Her own voice said crossly within her head: "He shouldn't have gone. He should never have left us."

The flaming hills of early October died abruptly. At last, the dreary rains of late fall turned into the first sputterings of snow until the world was beautiful once more with the silver branches of the bare trees and the lush tones of the evergreens against the gleaming banks of snow, so white you had to squint your eyes against it on a sunny day.

The master put the wagons and carriages in the shed and set Willie to cleaning the mud off wheels and undercarriages, and the sleds were brought out. The stagecoach came less often now. Though there was plenty of work to be done in the short winter days, there were not many guests to feed or look after. The few who came seemed as closed and secretive as the freezing grayness of the weather, bent on some narrow business of their own. "Slave catcher," Triphena was heard to mutter after one dark, sleekly well-dressed gentleman departed. "I don't like the smell of them."

If she had been home, she might have spent the dark afternoons spinning or sewing, but the mistress bought her woolens and calicoes at the village stores. She did not even card or spin the wool from their own sheep. It was sent to Nashua or Lowell, where it could be done in a gigantic water-powered mill. All the wealth that had once been Vermont's seemed to be trickling south or west. In fact, the master was heard to say that come spring, the sheep would be sold, because the western railroads were bringing such cheap wool to the Lowell factories that a New England sheep farmer could no longer compete.

It was what her own father had said, but his flock had been much smaller than Cutler's, so their family had felt the pinch years sooner.

One late morning, as she was peeling and cutting potatoes for the boiled noon meal, she felt a presence behind her shoulder. Then someone tweaked her right braid. She looked about, annoyed, expecting to say a sharp word to the bothersome Willie, when she saw it was Charlie.

She stood up, the knife and potato still in her hand. "Oh," she said. "Oh, you surprised me."

He was grinning. "I meant to," he said. "You look well."

"You're taller," she said, but it was a lie. He looked smaller than she remembered, but he would have been pained to hear that. "How are you, Charlie?" It wasn't a pleasantry, she really needed to know.

"Stil hopping," he said with a grin. "Work is slow in winter, so they let me come to see how you were."

Now that she was seeing him at last, she hardly knew what to say. "Have you heard anything from Mama and the babies?" she asked.

He shook his head. His hair was longer, but neater somehow. A better barber than she had trimmed it, she realized with a pang.

"You're busy," he said. "I don't mean to hinder you."

It was a stupid conversation. But both the cook and Willie were in the kitchen, and the mistress would be in and out. How could they say anything that mattered?

"Have you been to home at all?" she asked, turning back to her work and motioning him to sit on a low stool beside her.

"No," he said. "Nor you, ey?"

She shook her head. She wanted to tell him about the money. How she wanted to get it safely home. Ask him what she should do, but she couldn't, of course, with others about.

"I saw Luke a few times," he said. "He's been up once or twice to look at the farm. The house is fine." He lowered his voice. "He had a bit of a laugh about the way we blocked the door. He had to climb in the window."

She didn't like the idea of Luke or anyone else climbing in

the window. It made the cabin seem less secure. A coon or a bear might climb through the window as well, or a tramp. But she didn't comment.

"Do they work you hard?" she asked softly. He looked so small and thin.

"They're fair. The miller works as hard as any of us hands. The food is plenty and good."

Then why aren't you bigger? she wanted to ask him, but she held her tongue.

After he had gone, she thought of a hundred things she wished she had said. She could have told him about the frogs, if she'd remembered to. He would have laughed, and she longed to hear his laugh. She was much lonelier after he went. His presence for an hour had rubbed off some of her protection, leaving her feeling raw and exposed. He had left about noon, carrying some bread and cheese Triphena had pressed on him for his journey. He was wearing snowshoes that looked nearly as long as he was tall. Suppose it began to snow before he got back safely? Suppose he got lost? She tried to shake off her anxieties. Would someone let her know if something were to happen to him? It would be days, for they would let her mother know first, and then she might or might not write to Lyddie. It was too hard being separated like this. It was not right.

"The weather will hold, ey?" Triphena said, reading her mind. Lyddie sighed deeply. "You're worse than a little mother," the woman chided, but her eyes were softer than usual.

The weather did hold for another three days, and then the blizzard of the winter came. The stock was watered and fed, the cows were milked, but there was little that Otis and Enoch, the two hired men, could do outdoors, so the kitchen was crowded with men, seeking the warmth of the great fire as they made spills for the March sugaring, whittling four-inch segments of sumac, which they hollowed out with red-hot pokers. She thought of how she and Charlie had made spills last winter for tapping their own maples. Their own efforts were so childish compared to the practiced skill of these hired men.

She could hardly move in the kitchen, large as it was, without tripping over the gangly legs of a man or having one of them bar her path to the fireplace with a poker. Triphena grumbled continuously under her breath and rejoiced audibly when they left to tend to the livestock.

But Lyddie didn't mind so much. Their bodies were in the way of everything she had to do, but as they worked they talked, and the talk was a welcome window into the world beyond the tavern.

"They caught another slave up near Ferrisburg."

"The legislature can say all they want to about not giving up runaways, but as long as them rewards are high, somebody's going to report them."

"Well, you gotta decide." Enoch spat at the fire. His spit sizzled like fat on a hot griddle. "Who's in charge? Down in Washington slavery is the law of the land. Man buys a horse fair and legal, he sure as hell going after it if it bolts. You pay for something, it's yours. If the law says a man can own slaves, he's got a right to go after them if they bolt. Ain't no difference I can see."

"And if I happen to return somebody's property, seems to me I deserve a reward." Otis paused to pull his poker from the flames and thrust it smoking through the center of the sumac spill he held. "None of them high and mighty folks in Montpelier offered to pay me a hundred dollars *not* to report a runaway, now have they?"

"Well, this weather they likely to be froze 'fore you find 'em. You reckon the reward holds froze or thawed?"

"Why you suppose anyone'd try to run in winter? Don't they know how easy it is to track a critter in the snow?"

"Way I figure, it's not snowing down there where they come from, ey? They don't know what it's like up this way. They just see a chance to run, they run. They don't give it good thought."

I'd give it good thought, Lyddie said to herself. I'd get it all figured out close and choose my time right. If I was running, I'd pick me a early summer night with a lot of moon. I'd just travel by night, sleep in the day . . .

"Can you believe these fools?" Triphena was saying in her ear. "They don't know what it's like to be trapped."

Lyddie had never seen a black person. She tried to imagine how one might look and act. In a way, she'd like to see one, but what would she do? What would she say? And supposing it *was* a fugitive, what then? One hundred dollars! Would they really give you a hundred dollars for turning in a runaway slave? Surely, with that much money, she could pay off her father's debts and go back home.

March came. The sap began to rise in the sugar bush, and Cutler's was in a frenzy of activity. Willie went with the hired men to help in the gathering and boiling of the sap. Mr. Cutler had built a large sugaring shed two summers ago, and the only time any of the men were around the big house was when the livestock needed tending to. Even then, Lyddie was called on to help with the milking and the feeding and watering of the stock.

Added to all her other chores was the task of clarifying the syrup brought up to the house. They had never bothered much with clarifying at the farm as there had hardly been enough syrup or sugar for the family, but the mistress was very particular and stood over Lyddie directing her.

It was hot and exhausting work—beating milk and ash lye with the syrup and boiling the mixture until the impurities rose to the top in a scum and could be skimmed off—but the mistress, who only watched and commanded, declared the light, clear syrup worth the effort.

Some of the clarified syrup was boiled until it turned to sugar and was molded into fancy shapes. Lyddie's favorite among the lead molds was the head of George Washington, though sometimes the nose stuck and it was ruined.

It was because of the molded sugar that Lyddie's dream of taking the calf money home came true, though she couldn't have known how that dream was going to come out.

5

Going Home

By the second week of April, the sap had ceased to run, but it had been a good sugaring season. The mistress decided to take a large selection of the molded maple sugar to Boston. She could pay for her trip by selling the sugar, and it would give her a chance to see the big city and her perpetually ailing sister.

Work did not disappear with the departure of the mistress, but it became as pleasant as a holiday. "If I could make life so happy for others just by going away, I'd go more often," Triphena said. In two weeks Lyddie and Triphena and Willie, when they could catch him, turned the huge house inside out with scrubbing and cleaning. It smelled as good as the air of coming spring. And though there was a bit of fresh snow toward the end of the month, Lyddie knew it for the sham winter it was. Spring could not be denied forever.

"Well," said the cook one night. "The mistress earned herself a trip. I think the rest of us have, too."

"Where will you go, ey?" asked Lyddie wistfully.

"Me?" Triphena said. She was knitting and her worn red hands fairly flew over the yarn. "I got no place I want to visit. I been to Montpelier twice. That's enough. Boston's too big and too dirty. I wouldn't like it. Where would you go?"

"Home," said Lyddie, her voice no more than a whisper.

"Home? But that's hardly ten miles."

Lyddie nodded. It might as well be ten thousand.

"You can go and be back in no more than a couple of days at most."

What was the woman saying?

"Go on. Tomorrow, if you like."

Lyddie couldn't believe her ears. "But . . ."

"Who's going to care with the mistress gone?" She turned the row and began to purl without ever looking down.

"Would it be all right?"

"If I say so," Triphena said. "With her gone, I'm in charge, ey?" Lyddie wasn't going to argue. "If you was to wait, the ground would thaw to mud. Better go tomorrow if it's fair. Take a little sugar to your brother on the way."

Lyddie opened her mouth to ask again if it would be all right, but decided not to. If Triphena said she could go, who was Lyddie to question?

She was up before the sun, but she could tell the day would be a good one. She took a lunch bucket of bread and cheese and a little packet of molded sugar. The snow in the roadway was already turning to mud, and she slung a pair of snowshoes on her back in case the tracks up the mountain were still deep in snow.

She reached the mill in less than an hour, but to her disappointment Charlie was not there.

"I think he's off somewheres," one of the men said. "But you can ask up at the house."

A pretty, rather plump woman answered Lyddie's knock. "Yes?" she said, but she was smiling.

"I come to see Charles Worthen." Lyddie seemed to stumble over the words, which made her flush with embarrassment. "I'm his sister."

"Of course," the woman said. "Come in."

Lyddie stopped to leave her snowshoes and lunch bucket on the porch, then followed the woman into a large, fragrant kitchen. "I was just starting dinner," the woman said as if in apology as she hurried to stir the stew bubbling over the fire in the stone fireplace. "Charles is at school today." She replaced the lid on the kettle. "He's a very bright boy."

"Yes," said Lyddie. She would not be envious of Charlie. They were nearly the same person, weren't they?

"My husband is growing very fond of him."

What did she mean? Who was growing fond of Charlie? Charlie was not their child, not even their apprentice. She felt a need to explain to the woman that Charlie belonged to her, but she couldn't figure out how.

"Just tell him I was here, ey?" she said awkwardly. At the door she remembered the sugar and shoved it at the woman. "Some sugar," she mumbled.

"We'd be happy for you to stay awhile," the woman said, but Lyddie was already picking up her things. "I have to go," she said. "Not much time."

She realized later that she had forgotten to say thank you. But there was no going back. Besides she was in a hurry to get to the farm. She'd have time to clean the house well and check the roofs, as well as find a good place to hide the money. She'd just spend the night there, as it would be almost dark by the time she got everything done.

If she got an early start the next day, perhaps she could stop by once more at the mill . . . but, no . . . She couldn't stop by again and ask for Charlie and have him at school again. What would they think of her? And it might embarrass Charlie to have his sister clucking over him like an old biddy hen. She couldn't stand the thought of Charlie being mortified by her in front of these people who thought so highly of him.

Well, she was glad. Hadn't she felt bad that he didn't have a father and mother like Luke Stevens had to watch over him? But these weren't his real family. She was his real family. More than their mother, really, who had shucked them off like corn husks to follow her craziness.

Her anger, or whatever emotion it was that kept her head reeling, kept her feet moving as well. She was walking past the Stevenses' farm by noon. She never stopped to eat, but on the last leg of the trip she suddenly realized her hunger and chewed on the now hard roll and dry cheese as she climbed the narrow track toward the farm.

There was still plenty of snow on the track, but it was better packed than she had imagined. Mr. Westcott must be going back and forth to see to his cows. And then she realized there was snow on the pastures. There'd be no animals up in the fields. But of course—the sugaring. He had gone back and forth gathering sap from the sugar bush.

When she rounded the bend, she half expected the cabin to have disappeared. But there it sat, sagging a bit, squat and honest as her father had built it. The firewood was stacked against the door as she and Charlie had left it. The roofs seemed undamaged from the snow—thanks, perhaps, to Luke Stevens. Those must be his tracks around the cabin. She felt kindly toward the tall, awkward young Quaker for taking care.

She fetched the short ladder from the shed and propped it against one of the two south windows. Then she fetched a piece of split wood from the pile at the front door. The window should be easy to pry open unless it had swollen, but it hadn't. Indeed, it seemed to open quite smoothly, as though welcoming her home. Lyddie propped it up with the wood. She put her right leg over the sill and scrunched her head down onto her chest to squeeze into the opening.

Then she saw it at the fireplace—a shadowy form. She stifled a scream. "Luke?" she whispered. "That you?"

The form turned and stood up. She could barely make it out in the gloom of the cabin. It was a tall man. But not Luke. There was a strange man in her home—the whites of his eyes seemed enormous. And then she realized what was so strange about him. In the dim light his face and hands were very dark. Only his eyes shone. She was looking at a black man.

38

6

Ezekial

With one leg over the windowsill and her body pressed up under the window frame, there seemed no way to run. But why should she run? It was her house, after all, and what was one measly man, black or white, compared to a bear? Besides—she broke into a cold sweat—this man was likely to be worth one hundred dollars. Keeping her eyes on the intruder as though he *were* a bear, she managed to get her left foot across the sill and straighten herself to a sitting position on the window ledge. Pretending courage seemed to manufacture it, so she was just about to open her mouth to ask the man who he was and what he was doing in her house when he spoke to her.

"Verily, verily I say unto you, he that entereth not by the door but climbeth up some other way, the same is a thief and a robber." His voice was deep and smooth, almost like thick, brushed fur. She knew his words were from the Bible, but she was so astonished by the music of them that she sat there open-mouthed, unable to protest that whatever *he* might be, she was no thief.

"Never fear, little miss. My heart assures me that you're neither a thief nor a robber."

"No," she said, and then louder to show her authority, "I'm mistress here."

"Ah," he said, "we meet at last. You must be Miss Lydia Worthen, my hostess. Forgive my intrusion."

"How do you know my name, ey?" She had meant to ask his, or at least what he was doing in her house, but, as before, he'd gotten the better of her with his fancy talk and quick mind.

"Brother Stevens," he said. "He felt you would be understanding." He glanced at her, and for the first time since he had spied her at the window his expression seemed uncertain. "I hope he was not mistaken." He smiled apologetically. "Here, do come down from there and share a cup of tea with me. You've had a long journey, I'd imagine, and a rude shock, finding your home occupied by a stranger."

What else was she to do? She took the hand he held out to her, surprised by its roughness, as his skin looked like satin in the dim light.

He helped her to the floor. She followed as he led her to the rocker, and then she sat perched on the edge of the chair as he handed her a cup of birch tea. Why hadn't she spied smoke, coming up the road? But the man's fire was tiny, so perhaps there was none to see. The cabin was cold, though warmer than the outdoors. The man poured himself a cup and pulled up a stool on the other side of the fireplace to sit down facing her.

"You've come from the village," he said.

She nodded. The man could hardly be a runaway slave. He talked like a congregational preacher. But he was in hiding, that was plain.

"I should introduce myself," he said, reading her mind. "I'm Ezekial Abernathy, or was so called formerly. I was on the way northward when the snow delayed me last November."

Then he *was* a fugitive.

"I was conveyed to Brother Stevens's farm, where I stayed until it became clear that someone was watching their farm.

That was when young Luke spirited me here. He thought your log pile at the door would discourage curiosity."

"We done it to keep out wild critters."

"Yes," he said. "And you succeeded. I've been quite safe from wild ones here." He took a sip of his tea, keeping his eyes on the rim of the cup. "So far." He glanced up at her. "I would have left at once, but I was inconveniently ill. In the cold my lungs have been slow to clear."

"You talk like a preacher."

He relaxed a little. "Well, I am, or rather, I was."

"Then you ain't a slave?"

"Some have considered me a slave."

"But you talk nice." She hadn't meant to put it that way, but it came out unthought.

He smiled. "So do you."

"No," she said, "I mean you've had schooling—"

"I was my own schoolmaster," he said. 'At first I only wanted to read the Bible so I could preach to my people. But" —he smiled again, showing his lovely, even teeth—"a little reading is an exceedingly dangerous thing."

"Reading the Bible?"

"Especially the Bible," he said. "It gave me notions."

"So you just left, ey? Just set out walking?"

He leaned his head back, remembering. "Something like that," he said, but she could tell from his eyes that it was nothing like that at all.

"I couldn't leave my home," she said.

"No? And yet you did."

"I had no choice," she said hotly. "I was made to."

"So many slaves," he said softly.

"I ain't a slave," she said. "I just—I just—" Just what? "There was the debt my father left, so . . ." Whatever she said only made it seem worse. "But we own the land. We're free-men of the State of Vermont." He looked at her. "Well, my father is, or was, till he left, and my brother will be . . ." But Charlie was at school and living with strangers. She hated the man for making her think this way.

"I left the only home I knew," he said quietly. "I left a wife and child behind, vowing I would send for them or come for them within a few months. And here I sit, sick and penniless, hiding for my life, totally dependent on the kindnesses of others for everything." He shook his head and she was sorry she had had a moment's hate of him. Somewhere, perhaps, her father was saying those very same words.

After a while he stood up. "I can offer you a little rabbit stew," he said. "I'm afraid that's about all I have at the moment. Brother Luke will be coming up tonight with more food, I think, but if you're hungry—"

"I have some bread and cheese," she said.

"A veritable feast," he said, his good humor returned.

"When I first saw you"—they were eating and somehow she needed to let him know—"I . . . thought . . ." But she was ashamed to finish the sentence.

"It's a lot of money," he said gently. "I'd be tempted myself if I were you."

She could feel herself go hot and red. "But I won't," she said fiercely. "Now I know you, I couldn't ever."

"Thank you," he said. "A compliment as beautiful as the giver."

"It's dark in here," Lyddie said. "Or you could see I'm plain as sod."

"Or lovely as the earth." He used such fancy words, but she knew he wasn't using words to make fun of her.

Luke did come in the night, but she had slept so soundly that she didn't hear him. The proof was the odor of porridge bubbling over the fire when she awoke. She had slept in her clothes, and scrambled down the loft ladder at once.

"Ah, the sleeper awaketh!"

"It's late," she said. "I have to go." But he made her wait long enough to eat.

It was a strange good-bye. She did not hope to see Ezekial again. She hoped that he could cross the border fast as a fox—far away from the snares of those who would trap him. How could she have imagined for one minute that she could betray him? "I hope you get to Canada safe," she said. "And I hope your family can join you real soon." And then, without even thinking, she thrust her hand into her pocket and held out to him the calf-money bag. "You might need something along the way," she said.

The coins jangled as she passed them over.

"But this is yours. You'll need it. You earned it."

"No," she said. "I didn't earn it. It come from selling the calf. I was only going to bury it—till it was needed."

"Will you think of it as a loan, then?" he asked. "When I get established, I'll send it to you care of the Stevenses. With interest, if I can."

"There's no hurry. Wait till your family comes. I don't know when my brother and I can ever get back." She felt leaden with sadness. She pushed the stool to the window and climbed up. He held the window open as she climbed out. Someone—Luke perhaps—had left the short ladder in place.

"I can never thank you, my friend," Ezekial said.

"It was half Stevenses' calf by rights," she said, trying to diminish for both of them the enormity of what she had done. "It was their bull."

"I hope you find your freedom as well, Miss Lydia," he said. It wasn't until she was well down the road that she began to try to figure out what he had meant. And he was right. At Cutler's, despite Triphena's friendship, she was no more than a slave. She worked from before dawn until well after dark, and what did she have to show for it? She was no closer to paying

43

off the debt and coming home than she'd been a year ago. She needed cash money for that. She needed work that would pay and pay well. And there was only one place in New England where a girl could get a good cash wage for her work—and that was in Lowell, in the mills.

The weather held and the trip back was mostly downhill, so she was back by early afternoon. She hung the unused snowshoes in the shed and the lunch bucket in the pantry before she entered the warm kitchen.

"So! You've decided to honor us with a visit!" The mistress's face was red with heat or rage. Behind her, Triphena grimaced an apology.

She stood in the doorway, trying to frame an excuse or apology, but as usual the words did not come quickly enough to mind.

"You're dismissed!" the woman said.

"The best one you ever had," Triphena muttered.

"Unless—"

"No," Lyddie said quickly. "I know I done wrong to go off when you wasn't here. I'll just collect my things and be gone, ey?"

"You're wearing my dress!"

"Yes, ma'am. Shall I wash it before I go or—?"

"Don't be impertinent!"

Lyddie went past the angry woman without a word and up the back staircase to her tiny, windowless room. She pulled off the calico dress and put on the tight homespun, but it was like laying off a great burden. She felt more lighthearted than she had since the day Mrs. Peck brought the letter.

Triphena had followed her up. "Just stay out of sight today. By tomorrow she'll have come to her senses. She knows you're the best worker she's ever likely to get—and at no price at all.

Why she sends your mother fifty cents a week, and then, only if I remind her."

"I'm going to be a factory girl, Triphena."

"You what?"

"I'm free. She's set me free. I can do anything I want. I can go to Lowell and make real money to pay off the debt so I can go home."

"But your brother—"

"He'll be all right. He's in a good place where he's cared for. They're even letting him go to school."

"How can you get to Massachusetts? You've no money for coach fare."

"I'll walk," she said proudly. "A person should walk to freedom."

"A person's feet will get mighty sore," muttered Triphena.

7

South to Freedom

Lyddie set out at once. Or nearly at once. First Triphena made the girl put on her own second-best pair of boots. They were, of course, too large for Lyddie, so she had to wait while the cook fetched two extra pairs of stockings and paper with which to stuff the toes. When Lyddie objected, Triphena kept muttering, "A person can't walk to Massachusetts barefoot, not in April, she can't."

Next, Triphena made her wait while she packed her a parcel of food large enough to feed a table of harvesters. And, finally, she gave her a tiny cloth purse with five silver dollars in it.

"It's too much," Lyddie protested.

"I'm not having your dead body on my conscience," the cook said. "It will be enough for coach fare and the stops along the way. The only tavern food I trust is my own."

"But the mistress . . ."

"You leave the mistress to me."

"I'll pay you back the money—with interest when I can," Lyddie promised. Triphena only shook her head, and gave her a pat on the buttocks as though she were five years old.

"Just don't forget me, ey? Give your old friend a thought now and again. That's all the interest I'll be wanting."

It was three in the afternoon before she could even start her journey, but she would not let Triphena persuade her to wait.

She might let the mistress talk her into staying or lose her nerve if she didn't set out at once.

Her heart was light even if her feet felt clumsy in their makeshift boots and oversized stockings. She remembered Ezekial and thought: He walked north for freedom and I am walking south.

She had forgotten in the excitement that she had already walked above ten miles that day, but her feet remembered. Long before dark they were chafing in the unaccustomed bindings of stockings and ill-fitting boots, reminding her that they had done too much. She sat down on a rock and took the boots off. But before long she felt chilled, so she put them on again and started out, but more slowly than before.

Then, just at dusk, the sky opened, and it began to rain—not light spring showers, but cold, soaking torrents of rain, streaming down her face, icicling rivulets down her chest and legs.

She was obliged, reluctantly, to stop in the next village and seek shelter for the night. The mistress of the local inn was at first shocked to see a young girl traveling alone and then solicitous. "You look near drowned!" she cried, and asked her where she thought she was headed.

"Lowell, is it? Well, the stagecoach will be coming through the end of the week. Work for me till then and I'll give you your board."

Lyddie hesitated, but her sodden clothes and blistered feet reminded her how unsuited she was to continue the journey. She gratefully accepted the mistress's offer and worked so hard that before the week was out the woman was begging her to forget Lowell and stay on. But Lyddie was not to be persuaded.

She boarded the coach on Thursday in the same dismal rain she'd arrived in. Handing over three of her precious dollars to the driver, she settled herself in the corner of the carriage. There were only two other passengers—a man and a woman who seemed to be married, though they hardly spoke to each

47

other. The woman gave Lyddie's dress and shawl and strange boots a critical going over with her eyes, then settled again to her knitting, which the bumping of the coach made difficult.

With the muddy roads, it took two days to get to Windsor. They had not even left Vermont. Lyddie often wished she had saved her dollars and walked—rain or no rain. Surely she could have made it just as fast. But at least the disagreeable people left the coach at Windsor. The bed in the inn was infested with bugs, so she felt both filthy and itchy the next morning, and was not happily surprised that the coach, which had seemed overcrowded with three, was now to carry six as far as Lowell.

One of the passengers was a girl about her own age. Lyddie wanted to ask her if she, too, was going for a factory girl, but she had a young man with her who appeared to be her brother, so Lyddie was hesitant to speak. Then, too, she remembered the look the previous female passenger had given her.

The six of them were jammed into the carriage. There was hardly room for any of them to move, yet the rolling and pitching of the coach seemed worse rather than better for the load. Lyddie tried to sit delicately on one hip and then the other—to spread the bruising out if possible. One of the gentlemen lit a large pipe and the odor of it nearly made her retch. Fortunately, another gentleman reminded him sternly that there were ladies present, and the first man reluctantly tapped his pipe against the metal fixings of the door. But the stench had already been added to the air of foul breath and strong body odors. Lyddie longed for a healthy smell of a farmyard. People were so much fouler than critters.

And still, when the others weren't concentrating on keeping their seats in the swaying coach, they were looking at her—at her clothes especially. At first she was mortified, but the longer they rode, the angrier she became. How rude they were, these so-called gentry.

Everyone's clothes were a disgrace before they'd reached Lowell. The thaw and spring rains had turned parts of the roadway into muddy sloughs, and despite the coachman's skill, early on the last morning they were stuck fast. The passengers were all obliged to alight, and the four men ordered by the coachman to push the wheels out of the rut.

Lyddie watched the hapless gentlemen heave and shove and sweat, all to no avail. The coachman yelled encouragement from above. The men grunted and cursed below as their fancy breeches and overcoats turned brown with the mud and their lovely beaver hats went rolling off down the road.

After at least a quarter of an hour of watching, she could stand their stupidity no longer. Lyddie took off her worn shawl, tied it about her waist, and tucked up her skirts under it. She found a flat stone and put it under the mired wheel. Then she waded in, her narrow shoulders shoving two of the gaping men aside as she set her own strong right shoulder against the rear wheel, ordered the men to the rear boot, and called out; "One, two, three, heave!"

Above, she heard the laughter of the coachman. The men beside her were not smiling, but they did push together. The wheel rolled over the stone, and the coach was free to continue the journey.

She was filthy, but she hardly cared. She could only think of how ignorant, how useless her fellow passengers had been. None of them thanked her, but she hardly noticed. She was eager to be going, but not to ride inside. She looked up at the still smiling coachman. "Can I come up?" she called.

He nodded. Lyddie scrambled up beside him. None of the gentlemen offered her a hand, but she needed none, having spent her life climbing trees and ladders and roofs.

The coachman was still chuckling as he gave the horses a crack of the whip. Cries of protest rose up from the passengers below. He jerked the reins, his eyes twinkling, as more cries came up from the irate inmates as they tried to disentangle their bodies in the carriage and settle themselves on the seats once more.

He shook his head at Lyddie and held the pawing team for a few moments until the jostling in the carriage finally ceased. "You're a hardy one, you are," he said, reaching into the box behind him to pull out a heavy robe. "Here, this will keep the chill off."

She wrapped the robe around her head and body. "Silly fools," she said. "Not the common sense of a quill pig 'mongst the lot of them. Why didn't you tell them what to do, ey?"

"What?" he said. "And lose the entertainment?"

Lyddie couldn't help but laugh, remembering the sight of those sweating, swearing, filthy gentlemen, and now they were further poisoning the already stale air of the carriage with their odor and road mud. Indeed, someone was already raising the shade to let in a bit of cold, fresh air.

"So, you're for the factory life?"

Lyddie nodded. "I need the money."

He glanced sideways at her. "Those young women dress like Boston ladies," he said.

"I don't care for the fancy dress. There's debts on my farm . . ."

"And it's your farm, now is it?"

"My father's," she said. "But he headed West four years ago, and we haven't heard . . ."

"You're a stout one," he said. "Ain't you brothers to help?"

"One," she said. "And he'd be a great help, only my mother put him out to a miller, so until—"

"Have you someone to look out for you in Lowell? A relative, or a friend?"

She shook her head. "I'll do all right on my own."

"I've no doubt of that," he said. "But a friend to put in a word can't hurt. Let me take you to my sister's. She runs a boardinghouse, Number Five, it is, of the Concord Manufacturing Corporation."

"I'm obliged for your kindness, but—"

"Think of it as payment for your help."

"You could have had it out in no time, had you—"

"But never such fun. Coaching can be a wearisome, lonesome job, my girl. I take my pleasure where I can. Did you see those gentlemen's faces, having to be rescued by a slip of a farm girl?"

They crossed the bridge into the city late that afternoon. And city it surely was. It seemed to Lyddie that there were as many buildings crowded before her as sheep in a shearing shed. But they were not soft and murmuring as sheep. They were huge and foreboding in the gray light of afternoon. She would not have believed that the world contained as much brick as there was in a single building here. They were giants—five and six stories high and as long as the length of a large pasture. Chimneys, belching smoke, reached to the low hanging sky.

And the noise of it! Her impulse was to cover her ears, but she held her hands tightly in her lap. She would not begin to be afraid now, she who had stared down a bear and conversed easily with a runaway slave.

The other passengers in their muddy clothing and with their various trunks alighted at the Merrimack Hotel. Lyddie could tell at a glance it was too grand for her purse and person.

In the end, she waited until the coachman had seen the horses and carriage taken care of and then let him walk her to his sister's boardinghouse. "I've brought you a little chip of Vermont granite," he explained to the plump, smiling woman who met them at the door. Then he added, "We'd best come in by the back. Run into a little muddy stretch on the way down."

8

Number Five,
Concord
Corporation

At first she thought it was the bear, clanging the oatmeal pot against the furniture, but then the tiny attic came alive with girls. One struck a stick against a box, making the flash and odor of a tiny hell. And all this was just to light a candle that barely softened the predawn gloom of the attic. In the clatter of five girls dressing and squabbling over a single basin, Lyddie was forced fully awake and began to remember where she was.

Filthy as she had been, Mrs. Bedlow, the coachman's sister, had kindly taken her in. The boardinghouse keeper hurriedly gave her brother a cup of tea and sent him on his way. Then she had her son, a boy about Charlie's age, fill a tub of hot water in her own bedroom and ordered Lyddie to bathe. The mud-caked dress and shawl she carried away as soon as Lyddie shed them and plopped them directly in a pot of boiling water on the black iron cook stove.

And what a stove it was! Lyddie had only heard rumors of such modern wonders. When she came in from the boardinghouse keeper's bedroom, her face scrubbed barn red, her warm, lazy body straining every seam of her one remaining dress, the first thing her eyes lit upon was the stove. She stared at it as though it were an exotic monster from the depths of the sea. If she could have chosen, Lyddie would have pulled a chair close to it and felt its wonderful warmth and studied its marvels, but Mrs. Bedlow urged her into the dining room, which was soon filled with a noisy army of almost thirty young women, still full of energy after their long day in the factory. Lyddie's own head nearly settled into the plate of pork and beans, so that long before the others had finished, Mrs. Bedlow helped her up the four flights of stairs to the attic room, where she fell into bed hardly awake enough to mumble thanks for the woman's kindness.

And now, on this first morning of her new life, she lay in bed a few minutes to relish the quiet of the empty attic. Three days rattling in a coach, then to share a room with five others—indeed, a bed with a stranger who woke Lyddie in the middle of the night with her tossing and snoring—to be clanged awake by a bell, and to have her head punctured by shrieks and squeals and the rattle of voices—it made the windowless alcove she had left behind at Cutler's seem a haven of peace. But she would not look back. She threw off the quilt. She had nothing to wear but her much too small homespun. It couldn't be helped. She dressed herself and padded down the four flights of stairs in her darned and redarned stockings.

The front room was crowded with the two large dining tables that Tim, Mrs. Bedlow's son, was scurrying to set. Wonderful smells of coffee and apple pie and hash and—would it be fish?—wafted through the house from the magical stove as though to prove how many separate wonders it could perform at once.

"I've left my boots . . ." Lyddie started.

Mrs. Bedlow looked up, her round face radiant from the heat. "They're by the stove drying, but they won't do, you know."

"Ey?"

"Your clothes. Your boots. They simply won't do. That dress

is only fit now to be burned. Or what's left of it. I'm afraid it turned to mud stew in my kettle. What could my crazy brother have been thinking of letting a mere girl . . . ?"

"Oh, it wasn't his fault, ma'am," said Lyddie, slipping her feet into Triphena's boots, now stiff from a night beside the stove. "It was the men. They were so stupid . . ."

"You needn't tell me. I know that brother of mine. He was sitting up on top laughing, not giving a word of direction."

"But he had the coach and team . . ."

"Nonsense. He does it to amuse himself and humiliate his betters. He'd wreck a coach if he thought it would give him a rollicking story to tell in the tavern that night. And all at the cost of your clothes and dignity."

"Well, I ain't lost much either way."

"Have you any money at all?"

Lyddie hesitated. She really didn't. It was Triphena's money, not her own.

"If I'm to recommend you to the Concord Corporation, you need to look decent. They like to hire a good class of girls here."

Lyddie reddened.

"Of course, you're as good as anyone, a better worker than most, I suspect, but at the factory they'll look at your clothes and shoes to decide. The Almighty may look at the heart, but 'man looketh on the outward appearance' as the Good Book says, and that goes for women too, I fear. So you'll have to do better than . . ." She looked sadly at Lyddie's tight home-spun and stiff, worn boots.

Lyddie hung her head. "I have a bit left over from the trip. But it's on loan."

"You can pay it back after you're working. Now, would you like to give a hand? I think the girls will be home for breakfast early. The river's too high and the mill wheels are likely slowing. It means a holiday for them, but not for me."

Lyddie hastened to grab a cloth and take a pie Mrs. Bedlow

was removing from the bowels of the stove. "Yes," Mrs. Bedlow continued, "there'll be a few days off now till the water goes down." She smiled. "Time enough to get you proper clothes and a place in the factory as well."

If the girls had seemed noisy before, it was nothing compared to their entrance to breakfast. They burst through the door, each high-pitched voice shrieking to be heard over the others. There was an air of holiday that hardly paused for a blessing over the food and that erupted full blast before the echo of the "amen" died.

Lyddie, her feet alternately sloshing about and being pinched by Triphena's shoes, determinedly helped Tim serve both large tables. They brought in great platters of fried cod, hash, potato balls, pumpkin mush with huge pitchers of cream, toast and butter, apple pie, and pitchers of coffee and milk. Lyddie had never seen harvesters eat so much or so noisily. And these were supposed to be ladies.

"Hello, there," a voice cut through the din. "We didn't really meet you."

The room was suddenly quiet. "Don't be rude, Betsy," another said. "She was tired last night." Lyddie turned to see who had said this last because it was her idea of a lady's voice. The young woman who had spoken was smiling. "You only came in last night, didn't you, my dear?"

Lyddie nodded.

"There, don't be shy. We were all new once, even our Betsy." There was a titter from the rest. "I'm Amelia Cate." Her name was aristocratic—Amelia. It suited her. She was almost as pretty as the lady in pink that had come through the inn last year. Her skin was white and her face and hands long and delicate. And she was respected, or the others wouldn't have stopped chattering when she spoke.

"And you?"

"Lyddie Worthen. *Lydia* Worthen." With a rough finger she

scratched at the tight homespun across her chest. It seemed to Lyddie that the room was full of young women, all well-dressed, all delicate, all beautiful. And she a crow among peacocks.

"Vermont, isn't it?" said the one called Betsy, and a few of the others laughed.

"What's the matter with Vermont?" The voice had a bare trace of a Green Mountain twang. "I'm from near Rutland myself. Where do you hail from, Lyddie?"

Lyddie turned to see a girl not much older than herself, but, like all the others, whiter of complexion. She had light hair braided in a crown about her head and a serious face that a few freckles failed to relieve. Lyddie pulled at her own straggly brown plaits, grateful when attention shifted and the room was once again filled with chattering.

After breakfast, Amelia and the Rutland girl, whose name was Prudence Allen, offered to take her shopping for a proper dress, work apron, shoes, and bonnet. As they were leaving, Mrs. Bedlow pressed something into Amelia's hand, which turned out to be a dollar that Mrs. Bedlow claimed was a payment from her roguish brother for damages to Lyddie's clothing on the way.

Much to Lyddie's distress, it took all the money she had left, including the coachman's dollar, to dress her in a manner that satisfied Amelia and Prudence. She was so pained at the waste of money that she couldn't enjoy any of the new things, though she was pressed to wear the shoes home. In her heart she knew that she had never had a better-fitting pair—even the stiffness that she felt around the toes and heels and ankles was simply a reminder that she had on grand new city boots. When they were broken in, she would be able to walk anywhere in such shoes—even home.

Lyddie never quite knew how it was decided, but Mrs. Bedlow told her that evening that she would move her things from the attic to Amelia and Prudence's room on the third floor.

The other girls might grumble, which indeed they did, being passed over for a choice room by a newcomer, but Amelia had persuaded Mrs. Bedlow that since Lyddie had no relatives or friends in the house, indeed in the city, she needed their particular caring. Mrs. Bedlow, still feeling guilty about her brother, gave in. So Lyddie was moved to a smaller bedroom on the third floor to be with Amelia, Prudence, and the obviously disgruntled Betsy, who, since their previous roommate had gone home to New Hampshire the week before, had had the luxury of a bed to herself.

Four to a room was in itself a luxury, as most of the rooms held six. But even so, there was hardly any space to walk around the two double beds, the two tiny nightstands, and the various trunks and bandboxes of the inhabitants. There was no place to sit except on the beds, but then, on a regular workday there was no leisure time except the less than three hours between supper and curfew. Most of the girls spent their short measure of free time down in the parlor/dining room or out in town where there were shops and lectures and even dances, all run by honest citizens bent on parting the working girls from their wages.

"Now," said Amelia, who was far more conscientious about her duties as caretaker than Lyddie would have wished, "where will you be going to church on the Sabbath?"

Lyddie looked up in alarm. Living as far as they had from the village, the Worthens had never even bothered to pay pew rent in the village congregational church. "I—I hadn't thought to go."

Amelia sighed, reminding Lyddie that she was proving a harder case than the older girl had bargained for. "Oh, but you must," she said.

"What Amelia means," Betsy said, looking up from her novel, "is that regardless of the state of your immortal soul, the corporation requires regular attendance of all its girls. It makes us look respectable, even those of us who waste our precious minds on novels."

"Oh, do behave yourself, Betsy."

"Sorry, Amelia, but if I let you carry on about her moral duties when the girl plainly has no notion of them herself, this conversation will last all night." She put down her book and looked Lyddie straight in the face. "They'll probably make you put in an appearance from time to time somewhere. The Methodists don't press girls for pew rent, so if you're short on money, best go there. You have to pay for it in longer sermons, but nonetheless I always recommend the Methodists to new girls with no particular desire to go anywhere."

"Betsy!"

"Betsy likes to sound shocking," Prudence explained patiently. "Don't take it to heart." She was brushing out her long blonde hair and looked like a princess in a fairy tale, though her voice was far too matter-of-fact for a story book.

"But—" How should Lyddie explain it? "But, ain't Massachusetts a free country?"

"Of course, my dear," Amelia said. "But there are rules and regulations here as in any civilized establishment. They are meant for our own good, my dear. You'll see."

Betsy rolled her eyes and went back to her novel.

The next morning Mrs. Bedlow led Lyddie down the street past all the corporation boardinghouses to the bridge that led to the factory complex. Between two low brick buildings was a tall wooden fence. The gate of the fence was locked like a jail yard, but Mrs. Bedlow wasn't deterred. She simply went to the door of one of the low buildings and walked in. Lyddie followed, dragging her feet, for the room they entered was larger than the main floor of Cutler's Tavern, and it was crowded with tables and scriveners' desks. There were a few men working about the huge room, who looked up over their pens and account books as the two women passed, but it was clear that nothing much was being accomplished even in the counting room now that the water was too high to drive the mill wheel.

Mrs. Bedlow walked straight through the room and out the door on the opposite side into a courtyard large enough, it seemed to Lyddie, for the whole of their mountain farm to fit inside. The front gate and low south buildings—the counting house, offices, and storerooms, as Mrs. Bedlow explained—formed part of the enclosure. The two slightly shorter sides were taller frame structures—the machine shops and repair shops—and across the whole north end of the compound was the cotton mill itself—a gigantic six-story brick building. At one end ran the frame structure of the outdoor staircase. From the brick face, six even rows of windows seemed to glower down at her through the gray April drizzle like so many unfriendly eyes. A bell tower rose from the long roof, making the building seem even taller and more forbidding.

"It must seem imposing to a farm girl," Mrs. Bedlow said.

Lyddie nodded and tightened her grip on her shawl to keep from trembling.

Mrs. Bedlow turned back toward the low south building and knocked on a door marked "Agent."

"I've brought you a new girl," she said cheerily to the young man who opened the door. "Fresh from the farm and very healthy, as you can see."

The young man hardly gave Lyddie a glance, but stepped back and held the door for them to come in. "I'll see if Mr. Graves can spare a minute," he said haughtily.

"These clerks do put on airs," Mrs. Bedlow whispered, but if she was trying to make Lyddie feel more at ease, she failed. Nor was the sight of the agent himself any comfort.

"Mrs. Bedlow, isn't it?" He was a fat, prosperous-looking man, but without the manners to stand when a middle-aged lady came into his office.

Mrs. Bedlow talked very fast, her face flushed. Lyddie was sure the man would turn them both away—he looked barely patient as Mrs. Bedlow rattled on. But in the end, he said he would give Lyddie a contract for one year. There was a shortage in the weaving room at the moment. Mr. Thurston, the clerk, would give the girl the broadside with the regulations for the Concord and arrange for her to have her smallpox vaccination the following morning.

They were dismissed with a nod. Mrs. Bedlow punched Lyddie and prompted her to thank the agent for his kindness. Lyddie's voice could hardly manage a whisper, but it didn't matter. The gentleman wasn't paying her any attention.

She signed the paper where the clerk pointed, tried to listen carefully to all his warnings about what the contract demanded, and stuffed the broadside that he handed her into her apron pocket. She would study it tonight, she decided, her heart sinking. She could tell at a glance that it would be almost impossible for her to make out the meaning of such a paper. Oh, if only Charlie were here to read it aloud to her and explain the long words. Factory girls were not supposed to be ignorant, it would seem.

It would be several months before she could read with ease the "Regulations for the Boarding Houses of the Concord Corporation." But she found out the next day that it concealed unpleasant truths. The first of these was the vaccination. Mrs. Bedlow marched her over to the hospital after dinner where a doctor cruelly gouged her leg and poured a mysterious liquid directly into the wound.

Lyddie was even more distressed when the wound turned into a nasty sore in a few days' time, but she was only laughed at for her distress and told it was all for her own good. She'd never get the pox now, so she should be grateful. Amelia, indeed, was always instructing her to be grateful about things that Lyddie, try as she might, could not summon the least whiff of gratitude over. But finally, when she had been alternately shocked and bored for the better part of two weeks, the announcement was made at supper that work was to begin again the next day, and Lyddie felt a surge of gratitude that her days of idleness were over. She would be a true factory girl in a few hours' time.

Lyddie was mostly disappointed, but perhaps a tiny bit relieved, when Mrs. Bedlow announced that she would take her over to the weaving room after dinner. The large noonday meal must be out of the way and the dishes washed before the housekeeper could spare a moment, she said. Besides, it wouldn't do to be totally worn out the first day. Four hours would be plenty to start with.

The gate was locked. "They don't want tardy girls slipping past," Mrs. Bedlow explained. "You must always take care to be here when the bell rings." They entered the factory complex through the counting room as they had two weeks before, but this time it was teeming with men, all dressed like gentlemen. Every head seemed to rise, and every eye looked their way. Despite her new clothes, Lyddie could feel the shame burning through her rough brown cheeks. She ducked her bonneted head and hurried through as fast as she could, almost shoving Mrs. Bedlow in her haste.

Once in the yard, she was acutely aware of the thudding. The pulse of the factory boomed through the massive brick wall, and she could feel the vibrations of the machinery as they made their way up the shadowy wooden staircase, which clung for dear life to the side of the building.

Mrs. Bedlow huffed ahead, stopping more than once to catch her breath on the climb to the fourth floor. Once there, she jerked open the door, and the thudding beat exploded into a roar. She gave Lyddie a little push toward the racket. "Mr. Marsden is expecting you!" she yelled. "He'll see you settled in." And she was gone.

9

The Weaving Room

Creation! What a noise! Clatter and clack, great shuddering moans, groans, creaks, and rattles. The shrieks and whistles of huge leather belts on wheels. And when her brain cleared enough, Lyddie saw through the murky air row upon row of machines, eerily like the old hand loom in Quaker Stevens's house, but as unlike as a nightmare, for these creatures had come to life. They seemed moved by eyes alone—the eyes of neat, vigilant young women—needing only the occasional, swift intervention of a human hand to keep them clattering.

From the overarching metal frame crowning each machine, wooden harnesses, carrying hundreds of warp threads drawn from a massive beam at the back of each loom, clanked up and down. Shuttles holding the weft thread hurtled themselves like beasts of prey through the tall forests of warp threads, and beaters slammed the threads tightly into place. With alarming speed, inches of finished cloth rolled up on the beams at the front of the looms.

The girls didn't seem afraid or even amazed. As she walked by with the overseer, girls glanced up. A few smiled, some stared. No one seemed to mind the deafening din. How could they stand it? She had thought a single stagecoach struggling to hold back the horses on a downhill run was unbearably noisy. A single stagecoach! A factory was a hundred stagecoaches all inside one's skull, banging their wheels against the bone. Her impulse was to turn and run to the door, down the rickety stairs, through the yard and counting room, across the narrow bridge, past the row of boardinghouses, down the street—out of this hellish city and back, back, back to the green hills and quiet pastures.

But of course she didn't move a step. She didn't even cover her ears against the assault. She just stood quietly in front of the machine that the overseer had led her to and pretended she could hear what he was saying to her. His mouth was moving, a strange little red mouth peeping out from under his bushy black mustache. The luxuriant growth of the mustache was all the more peculiar because the overseer had hardly any hair on his head. His pate gleamed like polished wood.

Suddenly, to Lyddie's astonishment, the man put his red mouth quite close to her ear. She jerked her head away before she realized he was shouting the words: "Is that quite clear?"

Lyddie stared at him in terror. Nothing was clear at all. What did the man mean? Did he seriously think she could possibly have heard any of his mysterious mouthings? But how could she say she had heard nothing but the beastly racket of the looms? How could she say she could see hardly anything in the morning gloom of the huge, barnlike room, the very air a soup of dust and lint?

She was simply standing there, her mouth open with no words coming out, when an arm went around her shoulders. She shrank again from the touch before she saw it was one of the young women who tended the looms. Her head was close enough to Lyddie's left ear so that Lyddie could hear her say to the overseer, "Don't worry, Mr. Marsden, I'll see she settles in."

The overseer nodded, obviously relieved not to have to deal with Lyddie or the loom he'd assigned her.

"We'll work together," the girl shouted in her ear. "My

two machines are just next to you here. I'm Diana." She motioned for Lyddie to stand close behind her right shoulder, so although Lyddie wasn't in her way as she worked, the older girl could speak into Lyddie's left ear by turning her head slightly to the right.

Suddenly, Diana banged a metal lever at the right of the machine and the loom shivered to a halt. At either end of the shed, made by the crisscrossing of warp threads, was a narrow wooden trough. From the trough on the left she retrieved the shuttle. The shuttle was wood, pointed and tipped at either end with copper. It was about the shape of a corncob, only a little larger and hollowed out so that it could carry a bobbin or quill of weft thread. With her hands moving so quickly that Lyddie could hardly follow them, Diana popped out a nearly empty quill of thread and thrust in a full one from a wooden box of bobbins near her feet. Then she put her mouth to a small hole near one end of the shuttle and sucked out the end of the weft thread.

"We call it the kiss of death," she shouted, smiling wryly to soften the words. She pulled out a foot or more of the thread, wound it quickly around one of two iron hooks, and rehung the hooks into the last row of woven cloth. The hooks were attached by a yard or so of leather cord to a bell-shaped iron weight. "You have to keep moving your temple hooks," Diana said. "Pulls the web down snug as you go." She pointed to the new inches of woven fabric.

"Now," said Diana, speaking into Lyddie's ear, "make sure the shuttle is all the way at the end of the race—always on your right here." She placed the shuttle snug against the right-hand end of the trough. "We don't want any flying shuttles. All right, then, we're ready to go again." Diana grasped the metal lever, pulled it toward the loom, and jammed it into a slot. The loom shuddered once more to life.

For the first hour or so Lyddie watched, trying mostly to

64

stay out of Diana's way as she moved among the three machines, two opposite and one adjoining. The older girl refilled the shuttles when they ran low and rehung the temple hooks to keep the web tight. Then, without warning, for no reason that Lyddie could see, Diana slammed off one of the looms.

"See," she said, pointing at the shed, "a warp thread's snapped. If we don't catch that, we're in trouble." An empty shuttle might damage a few inches of goods, she explained, but a broken warp could leave a flaw through yards of cloth. "We don't get paid when we ruin a piece." She pinched a tiny bag hung from the metal frame of the loom. It spit out a puff of talc, which she rubbed into her fingertips. Then fishing out the broken ends of warp, she showed Lyddie how to fasten them together with a weaver's knot. When Diana tied the ends, they seemed to melt together, leaving the knot invisible. She stepped aside. "Now you start it," she said.

Lyddie was a farm girl. She took pride in her strength, but it took all of her might to yank the metal lever into place. She broke into a sweat like some untried plow horse. The temples were not much larger than apples, but when Diana asked her to move one, she felt as though someone had tied a gigantic field stone to the end of the leather cord. Still, the physical strength the work required paled beside the dexterity needed to rethread a shuttle quickly, or, heaven help her, tie one of those infernal weaver's knots.

Everything happened too fast—a bobbin of weft thread lasted hardly five minutes before it had to be replaced—and it was painfully deafening. But tall, quiet Diana moved from loom to loom like the silent angel in the lion's den, keeping Daniel from harm.

There were moments when all three looms were running as they ought—all the shuttles bearing full quills, all three temples hung high on the cloth, no warp threads snapping. During one of these respites, Diana drew Lyddie to the nearest window.

The sill was alive with flowers blooming in pots, and around the frame someone had pasted single pages of books and magazines. Diana pressed down a curling corner of a poem. Most of the sheets were yellowing. "Not so much time to read these days," Diana said. "We used to have more time. Do you like to read, Lyddie?"

Lyddie thought of the regulations that she was still trying laboriously to decipher when no one was looking. "I've not much schooling."

"Well, you can remedy that," the older girl said. "I'll help, if you like, some evening."

Lyddie looked up gratefully. She felt no need with Diana to apologize or to be ashamed of her ignorance. "I'm needing a bit of help with the regulations . . ."

"I shouldn't wonder. They're a trial for us all," Diana said. "Why don't you bring the broadside over to Number Three tonight and we'll slog through that wretched thing together."

Amelia was not pleased that evening after supper when she realized that Lyddie was getting ready to go out. "Your first day. You ought to rest."

"I'm all right," said Lyddie. And, indeed, once the noise of the weaving room was out of her ears, she did feel quite all right. A bit tired, but certainly not overweary. "I aim to do a bit of studying," she said. It made her feel proud to say such a thing.

"Studying? With whom?"

"The girl I'm working with in the weaving room. Diana—" She realized that she didn't know Diana's surname.

Amelia, Prudence, and Betsy worked in the spinning room on the third floor, so she supposed they did not know Diana. Betsy looked up from her ever-present novel. "Diana Goss?" she asked.

"I don't know. Just Diana. She was very kind to me today."

"Diana Goss?" echoed Amelia. "Oh Lyddie, don't be taken in."

Lyddie couldn't believe her ears. "Ey?"

"If it's Diana Goss," Prudence said, "she's a known radical, and Amelia is concerned—"

"Ey?"

Betsy laughed. "I don't think our little country cousin is acquainted with any radicals, known or unknown."

"I know Quakers," Lyddie said. "Creation! They're abolitionists, every one, ey?"

"Hoorah for you." Betsy put down her novel and made a little show of clapping her hands.

Amelia was sewing new ribbons on her Sunday bonnet and, watching Betsy's performance, managed to jab the needle into her finger instead of the hat brim. She stuck her finger in her mouth and looked up annoyed. "I wish you wouldn't keep saying things like 'creation' and 'ey,' Lyddie. It's so—so—"

"Only the *new* girls from Vermont speak like that," said Prudence, whose own mountain speech was well tamed.

Lyddie didn't quite know what to do. She had no desire to anger her roommates, but she was quite set on going to see Diana. It wasn't just the foolish regulations. She wanted to learn everything—to become as quietly competent as the tall girl. She knew enough about factory life already to realize that good workers in the weaving room made good money. It wasn't like being a maid where hard work only earned you a bonus in exhaustion.

"Well," she said, tying her bonnet, "I'll be back soon."

"I'd rather you wouldn't go at all," Amelia said coolly.

Lyddie smiled. She didn't mean to seem unfriendly or even ungrateful, though it was tiresome to be always beholden to Amelia. "I don't want you to worry after me. I'm able to do for myself, ey?"

"Hah!" Betsy's short laugh came out like a snort.

"It's just—" Prudence said "—it's just that you haven't been here long enough to know about certain things. Amelia doesn't—well, none of us—want you to find yourself in an awkward situation."

For a moment Lyddie was afraid that Amelia or even Prudence would start in to lecture her, so she grabbed her shawl and said as she was moving out of the bedroom door, "I'll watch out." Though what she was promising to look out for, she had no idea.

Diana's boardinghouse was only two houses away from her own. The architecture was identical—a four-story brick building—lined with rows of windows that blinked like sleepy eyes as lamps and candles were lit against the dusk of an April evening.

The front door was unlocked, so she walked into the large front room, like Mrs. Bedlow's, nearly filled with two large dining tables but with the semblance of a living area on one side. And just as in Mrs. Bedlow's parlor, chairs had been pulled away from the tables and girls were chatting and sewing and reading in the living area. It was as noisy and busy as a chicken yard. Peddlers had come off the street to tempt the girls with ribbons and cheap jewelry. A local phrenologist was in one corner measuring a girl's skull and preparing to read her character from his findings. Several girls were watching this consultation transfixed.

Lyddie pushed the door shut but stood just inside, uncertain how to proceed. How could she ask for Diana when she wasn't even sure of her proper name?

But she needn't have worried. Out of the chattering mass of bodies, Diana rose from her chair in the corner and came to where Lyddie stood. She smiled and her long, serious face creased into dimples. "I'm so glad you came. Let's go upstairs where we can speak in something less than a shout."

What a relief it was to climb the stairs and leave most of

the racket two floors behind. There was no one else in Diana's room. "What a treat," Diana said, as though reading Lyddie's mind. "Sometimes I'd sell my soul for a moment of quiet, wouldn't you?"

Lyddie nodded. She suddenly felt shy around Diana, who seemed even more imposing away from the looms when her lovely, elegant voice was pitched rich and low like the call of a mourning dove.

"First, we need to get properly introduced," she said. "I'm Diana Goss." She must have noted a flicker of something in Lyddie's face, because she added, "The *infamous* Diana Goss," and dimpled into her lovely smile.

Lyddie reddened.

"So you've been warned."

"Not really—"

"Well, then, you will be. I'm a friend of Sarah Bagley's." She watched Lyddie's face for a reaction to the name, and when she got none tried another. "Amelia Sargeant? Mary Emerson? Huldah Stone? No? Well, you'll hear those names soon enough. Our crime has been to speak out for better working conditions." She looked at Lyddie again. "Yes, why, then, should the operatives themselves fear us? It is, dear Lyddie, the nature of slavery to make the slave fear freedom."

"I'm not a slave," Lyddie said, more fiercely than she intended.

"You're not here for a lecture. I'm sorry. Tell me about yourself."

It was hard for Lyddie to talk about herself. She'd had no practice. With Amelia and Prudence and Betsy, she didn't need to. They—especially Amelia—seemed always to be telling her about herself or trying to make her like themselves. Besides, what was interesting about her? What would someone like Diana want to know?

"There's Charlie," she began. And before she knew it, she

69

was explaining that she was here to earn the money to pay off her father's debts, so she and Charlie could go home.

Diana did not smile ironically or laugh as Betsy was sure to. She did not once lecture her as though she were a slow child the way Amelia often did—or offer a single explanation as Prudence would have felt obliged to. No, the tall girl perched on the edge of a bed and listened silently and intently until Lyddie ran out of story to tell. Lyddie was a bit breathless, never having said so many words in the space of so few minutes in her life. And then, embarrassed to have talked so long about herself, she asked, "But I reckon you know how it is with families, ey?"

"Not really. I can hardly remember mine. Only my aunt that kept me until I was ten. And she's gone now."

Lyddie made as if to sympathize, but Diana shook it off. "I think of the mill as my family. It gives me plenty of sisters to worry about. But," she said, "I don't think I need to worry about you. You don't know what it is *not* to work hard, do you?"

"I don't mind work. The noise—"

Diana laughed. "Yes, the noise is terrible at the beginning, but you get accustomed to it somehow."

Lyddie found that hard to believe, but if Diana said so . . .

"And I don't suppose you think a thirteen-hour day overly long, either."

Lyddie's days had never been run on clocks. "I just work until the work is done," she said. "But I never had leave to go paying calls in the evenings before."

"And the wages seem fair?"

"I ain't been paid yet, but from what I hear—"

"What did you get at the inn?"

"I don't know. Fifty cents the week, I think. They sent it to Mama. Triphena said the mistress was like to forget as not.

70

I suppose Charlie—" Lyddie stopped speaking. Neither Charlie nor her mother knew where she was!

"Is something the matter, Lyddie?"

"I haven't wrote them. Charlie nor my mother. They don't know where I am." Suppose they needed her? How would they find her? Lyddie felt the panic rising. She was cut off from them all. She might as well have gone to the other side of the world. She was out of their reach. "When will they pay me?"

"If it's paper you need—"

"It's postage, too. I'd have to prepay. They don't have the money to pay at that end."

"I could manage postage."

"I can't borrow. I borrowed too much already."

But Diana quietly insisted. Lyddie owed it to her family to let them know right away, she said. She brought out paper, pen and ink, and a sturdy board for Lyddie to write upon. Lyddie would have felt shy about forming her letters so laboriously in front of Diana, but Diana took up a book and made Lyddie feel as though she were alone.

Dear Mother,
    You will be surprize to no I am gone to Lowell to work. I am in the weving rum at the Concord Corp. I bord at number 5 if you rit me. Everwun is kind and the food is plenty and tasty. I am saving my muny to pay the dets.
    I am well. I trus you and the babbies are well to.

Yr. fathfull dater,
Lydia Worthen

It seemed extravagant to take another sheet to write to Charlie, but Diana had said that she ought to write to him as well.

Dear Bruther,
    Do not be surprize. I am gone to Lowell for a factry girl.

Everwun is kind. The work is alrite, but masheens is nosy, beleev me. The muny is good. I will save and pay off the dets. So we can stil hop. (Ha ha)

Yr. loving sister,
Lydia Worthen

P.S. I am at Concord Corp. Number 5 if you can rit. Excuse al mistaks. I am in grate hurry.

She folded the letters, sealed them with Diana's wax, and addressed them. Before she could ask further about posting them, Diana took the letters from her hand. "I have to go tomorrow anyhow. Let me mail them for you."

"I'll pay you back as soon as I get paid." She sighed. "As soon as I pay Triphena—"

"No," said Diana. "This time it's my welcoming gift. You mustn't try to repay a gift."

The bell rang for curfew. "We haven't looked at the silly regulations," Diana said. "Well, another time . . ."

Diana walked her to Number Five. It was a bright, cool night, though in the city, the stars seemed dim and far away. "Until tomorrow," Diana said at the door.

"I'm obliged to you for everything," Lyddie said.

Diana shook her head. "They need to know. They'll worry."

The roommates were already getting into bed. "You're late," Amelia said.

"I come as soon as the bell rung—"

"Oh, you're not really late," said Betsy. "Amelia just doesn't approve of where you've been."

"It *was* Diana Goss, wasn't it?" Amelia asked.

"Yes."

"And?" Lyddie was taking off her bonnet, then her shawl. And what? What did Amelia mean? Amelia answered her own question. "Did she try to make you join?"

Lyddie folded her shawl, still uncomprehending.

"She means," said Betsy, "did she tie you up and torture

72

you until you promised to join the Female Labor Reform Association?"

"Oh, Betsy," said Prudence.

"She never mentioned such," Lyddie said. She made her way around Amelia and Prudence's bed and trunks to the side of the bed that she shared with Betsy. She sat on the edge and began to take off her shoes and stockings.

"Then what were you doing all that time?"

Betsy slammed her book shut. "What affair is it of yours, Amelia?"

"It's all right," Lyddie said. She had no desire to get her roommates stirred up over nothing. "She just give me paper to write to my family to tell them where I was."

"Oh Lyddie," Prudence said. "How thoughtless of us. We never offered."

"No matter," Lyddie said. "I done it now."

"She's devious," Amelia muttered. "You have to watch her. Believe me, Lyddie. I'm only thinking of your own good."

Betsy snorted, reached over, and blew out the candle as the final curfew bell began to clang.

10
Oliver

The four-thirty bell clanged the house awake. From every direction, Lyddie could hear the shrill voices of girls calling to one another, even singing. Someone on another floor was imitating a rooster. From the other side of the bed Betsy groaned and turned over, but Lyddie was up, dressing quickly in the dark as she had always done in the windowless attic of the inn.

Her stomach rumbled, but she ignored it. There would be no breakfast until seven, and that was two and a half hours away. By five the girls had crowded through the main gate, jostled their way up the outside staircase on the far end of the mill, cleaned their machines, and stood waiting for the workday to begin.

"Not too tired this morning?" Diana asked by way of greeting.

Lyddie shook her head. Her feet were sore, but she'd felt tireder after a day behind the plow.

"Good. Today will be something more strenuous, I fear. We'll work all three looms together, all right? Until you feel quite sure of everything."

Lyddie felt a bit as though the older girl were whispering in church. It seemed almost that quiet in the great loom room. The only real noise was the creaking from the ceiling of the leather belts that connected the wheels in the weaving room to the gigantic waterwheel in the basement.

The overseer came in, nodded good morning, and pushed a low wooden stool under a cord dangling from the assembly of wheels and belts above his head. His little red mouth pursed, he stepped up on the stool and pulled out his pocket watch. At the same moment, the bell in the tower above the roof began to ring. He yanked the cord, the wide leather belt above him shifted from a loose to a tight pulley, and suddenly all the hundred or so silent looms, in raucous concert, shuddered and groaned into fearsome life. Lyddie's first full day as a factory girl had begun.

Within five minutes, her head felt like a log being split to splinters. She kept shaking it, as though she could rid it of the noise, or at least the pain, but both only seemed to grow more intense. If that weren't trial enough, a few hours of standing in her proud new boots and her feet had swollen so that the laces cut into her flesh. She bent down quickly to loosen them, and when she found the right lace was knotted, she nearly burst into tears. Or perhaps the tears were caused by the swirling dust and lint.

Now that she thought of it, she could hardly breathe, the air was so laden with moisture and debris. She snatched a moment to run to the window. She had to get air, but the window was nailed shut against the April morning. She leaned her forehead against it; even the glass seemed hot. Her apron brushed the pots of red geraniums crowding the wide sill. They were flourishing in this hot house. She coughed, trying to free her throat and lungs for breath.

Then she felt, rather than saw, Diana. "Mr. Marsden has his eye on you," the older girl said gently, and put her arm on Lyddie's shoulder to turn her back toward the looms. She pointed to the stalled loom and the broken warp thread that must be tied. Even though Diana had stopped the loom, Lyddie stood rubbing the powder into her fingertips, hesitating to plunge her hands into the bowels of the machine. Diana urged her with a light touch.

I stared down a black bear, Lyddie reminded herself. She

took a deep breath, fished out the broken ends, and began to tie the weaver's knot that Diana had shown her over and over again the afternoon before. Finally, Lyddie managed to make a clumsy knot, and Diana pulled the lever, and the loom shuddered to life once more.

How could she ever get accustomed to this inferno? Even when the girls were set free at 7:00, it was to push and shove their way across the bridge and down the street to their boardinghouses, bolt down their hearty breakfast, and rush back, stomachs still churning, for "ring in" at 7:35. Nearly half the mealtime was spent simply going up and down the staircase, across the mill yard and bridge, down the row of houses—just getting to and from the meal. And the din in the dining room was nearly as loud as the racket in the mill—thirty young women chewing and calling at the same time, reaching for the platters of flapjacks and pitchers of syrup, ignoring cries from the other end of the table to pass anything.

Her quiet meals in the corner of the kitchen with Triphena, even her meager bowls of bark soup in the cabin with the seldom talkative Charlie, seemed like feasts compared to the huge, rushed, noisy affairs in Mrs. Bedlow's house. The half hour at noonday dinner with more food than she had ever had set before her at one time was worse than breakfast.

At last the evening bell rang, and Mr. Marsden pulled the cord to end the day. Diana walked with her to the place by the door where the girls hung their bonnets and shawls, and handed Lyddie hers. "Let's forget about studying those regulations tonight," she said. "It's been too long a day already."

Lyddie nodded. Yesterday seemed years in the past. She couldn't even remember why she'd thought the regulations important enough to bother with.

She had lost all appetite. The very smell of supper made her nauseous—beans heavy with pork fat and brown injun bread with orange cheese, fried potatoes, of course, and flapjacks with apple sauce, baked Indian pudding with cream and plum cake for dessert. Lyddie nibbled at the brown bread and washed it down with a little scalding tea. How could the others eat so heartily and with such a clatter of dishes and shrieks of conversation? She longed only to get to the room, take off her boots, massage her abused feet, and lay down her aching head. While the other girls pulled their chairs from the table and scraped them about to form little circles in the parlor area, Lyddie dragged herself from the table and up the stairs.

Betsy was already there before her, her current novel in her hand. She laughed at the sight of Lyddie. "The first full day! And up to now you thought yourself a strapping country farm girl who could do anything, didn't you?"

Lyddie did not try to answer back. She simply sank to her side of the double bed and took off the offending shoes and began to rub her swollen feet.

"If you've got an older pair"—Betsy's voice was almost gentle—"more stretched and softer . . ."

Lyddie nodded. Tomorrow she'd wear Triphena's without the stuffing. They were still stiff from the trip and she'd be awkward rushing back and forth to meals, but at least there'd be room for her feet to swell.

She undressed, slipped on her shabby night shift, and slid under the quilt. Betsy glanced over at her. "To bed so soon?"

Lyddie could only nod again. It was as though she could not possibly squeeze a word through her lips. Betsy smiled again. She ain't laughing at me, Lyddie realized. She's remembering how it was.

"Shall I read to you?" Betsy asked.

Lyddie nodded gratefully and closed her eyes and turned her back against the candlelight.

Betsy did not give any explanation of the novel she was reading, simply commenced to read aloud where she had broken off reading to herself. Even though Lyddie's head was still choked with lint and battered with noise, she struggled to get the sense of the story.

The child was in some kind of poorhouse, it seemed, and he was hungry. Lyddie knew about hungry children. Rachel, Agnes, Charlie—they had all been hungry that winter of the bear. The hungry little boy in the story had held up his bowl to the poorhouse overseer and said:

"Please sir, I want some more."

And for this the overseer—she could see his little rosebud mouth rounded in horror—for this the overseer had screamed out at the child. In her mind's eye little Oliver Twist looked exactly like a younger Charlie. The cruel overseer had screamed and hauled the boy before a sort of agent. And for what crime? For the monstrous crime of wanting more to eat.

"That boy will be hung," the agent had prophesied. "I know that boy will be hung."

She fought sleep, ravenous for every word. She had not had any appetite for the bountiful meal downstairs, but now she was feeling a hunger she knew nothing about. She had to know what would happen to little Oliver. Would he indeed be hanged just because he wanted more gruel?

She opened her eyes and turned to watch Betsy, who was absorbed in her reading. Then Betsy sensed her watching, and looked up from the book. "It's a marvelous story, isn't it? I saw the author once—Mr. Charles Dickens. He visited our factory. Let me see—I was already in the spinning room—it must have been in—"

But Lyddie cared nothing for authors or dates. "Don't stop reading the story, please," she croaked out.

"Never fear, little Lyddie. No more interruptions," Betsy promised, and read on, though her voice grew raspy with fatigue, until the bell rang for curfew. She stuck a hair ribbon in the place. "Till tomorrow night," she whispered as the feet of an army of girls could be heard thundering up the staircase.

11

The Admirable Choice

The next day in the mill, the noise was just as jarring and her feet in Triphena's old boots swelled just as large, but now and again she caught herself humming. Why am I suddenly happy? What wonderful thing is about to happen to me? And then she remembered. Tonight after supper, Betsy would read to her again. She was, of course, afraid for Oliver, who was all mixed up in her mind with Charlie. But there was a delicious anticipation, like molded sugar on her tongue. She had to know what would happen to him, how his story would unfold.

Diana noticed the change. "You're settling in faster than I thought," she said. But Lyddie didn't tell her. She didn't quite know how to explain to anyone, that it wasn't so much that she had gotten used to the mill, but she had found a way to escape its grasp. The pasted sheets of poetry or Scripture in the window frames, the geraniums on the sill, those must be some other girl's way, she decided. But hers was a story.

As the days melted into weeks, she tried not to think how very kind it was of Betsy to keep reading to her. There were nights, of course, when she could not, when there was shopping or washing that had to be done. On Saturday evenings they were let out two hours early and Amelia corralled Lyddie and Prudence for long walks along the river before it grew too dark. Betsy, of course, did whatever she liked regardless of

Amelia. Sundays Amelia dragged the reluctant Lyddie to church. At first Lyddie had been afraid Betsy would go on reading without her, but Betsy waited until Sunday afternoon, when Amelia and Prudence were down in the dining room writing their weekly letters home, and she picked up the story just where she had stopped on the previous Friday evening.

It was several weeks before Lyddie caught on that the novel was from the lending library and thus cost Betsy five cents a week to borrow. On her own, Betsy could have read it much faster, Lyddie was sure of that. As much as she hated to spend the money, on her first payday, Lyddie insisted on giving Betsy a full ten cents to help with *Oliver*'s rent. Betsy laughed, but she took it. She, too, was saving her money, she confessed quietly to Lyddie and asked her not to tell, to go for an education. There was a college out West in Ohio that took female students—a real college, not a young ladies' seminary. "But don't tell Amelia," she said, her voice returning to its usual ironic tone, "she'd think it unladylike to want to go to Oberlin."

It seemed strange to Lyddie that Betsy should care at all what Amelia thought. But Lyddie, who had never had any ambition to be thought a lady, did find herself asking, What would Amelia think?—and censoring her own behavior from time to time accordingly.

Then, all too soon, the book was done. It seemed to have flown by, and there was so much, especially at the beginning—when Lyddie was too tired and, try as she might, could not listen properly—so much at the beginning that she needed to hear again. Actually, she needed to hear the whole book again, even the terrible parts, dear Nancy's killing and the death of Sikes.

She wished she dared to ask Betsy to read more, but she could not. Betsy had given her hours and hours of time and voice. And besides, with July nearly upon them, the three roommates were making plans for going home. The very word was like a blow to her chest. Home. If only she could go. But she had signed with the corporation for a full year of work. If she left, even just to see the cabin and visit for an hour or so with Charlie, she would lose her position. "And if you leave without an honorable discharge," the clerk had said, "not only will you never work at the Concord Corporation again, but no other mill in Lowell will ever engage you." Blacklisted! The word sent chills down her backbone.

So she watched her roommates pack their trunks and listened as they chattered about whom they would see and what they would do, and tried not to mind. Amelia would go to New Hampshire where her clergyman father had a country church. Her mother would welcome her help around the manse and with the tutoring of the farm children in the parish Sunday School. Prudence was bound for the family farm near Rutland, where, Amelia hinted, a suitor on a neighboring farm was primed to snatch her away from factory life forever. Betsy's parents were dead, but there was an uncle in Maine who was always glad for her to come and help with the cooking. Haying season would soon be here, and there would be many mouths to feed. There was a chance, as well, Betsy said, of seeing her brother. But again, he might be too pressed with invitations from his university mates to find time for a visit with a sister who was only an old spinster and a factory girl to boot.

After they are gone, I will be earning and saving, Lyddie said to comfort herself. I may earn even more. If the weaving room is short of workers, Mr. Marsden may assign me another loom. Then I could turn out many more pieces each week. For she was proficient now. Weeks before she had begun tending her own loom without Diana's help.

She hadn't imagined that Diana would go on holiday as well, but when Diana told her she was going, she felt a little thrill. Mr. Marsden was sure to give her charge of at least two looms, perhaps a third. She didn't want Diana to think she was rejoicing in her absence, but she was not skilled at feigning feelings she did not own. "I'll miss you," she said.

Diana laughed at her. "Oh, you'll be glad enough to see me gone," she said. "There'll be three looms for you to tend, a nice fat raise to your wages for these several weeks." Lyddie blushed. "You needn't feel bad. Enjoy the money. I think you'll find you've earned every penny. It's hot as Hades up here in July."

"But where will you be going?" Lyddie asked, trying to shift attention from herself. She quickly repented, remembering too late that Diana had no family waiting to see her.

"It's all right," Diana said in reply to Lyddie's pained look. "I was orphaned young. I'm used to it. I suppose this mill is as much home as I can claim. I started here as a doffer when I was ten. So I've fifteen years here. But only a scant handful of Julys."

Lyddie wanted to ask, then, if she had no home to go to, where she was headed, but it wasn't rightly her business, and Diana didn't offer the information except to say when the noise of the machines insured that no one could overhear, "There'll be a mass meeting at Woburn on Independence Day." When Lyddie looked puzzled, she went on, "Of the movement. The ten-hour movement. Miss Bagley will speak, as well as some of the men." When Lyddie still said nothing, she continued, "There'll be a picnic lunch, a real Fourth of July celebration. How about it? I promise no one will make you sign your name to anything."

Lyddie pressed her lips together and shook her head. "No," she said. "I expect I'll be busy."

July was hot, as Diana had so inelegantly predicted. Reluctantly, Lyddie spent a dollar on a light summer work dress as her spring calico proved unbearable. Her other expenditure was at the lending library, where she borrowed *Oliver Twist.*

This time she would read it on her own. It didn't occur to her that she was teaching herself as she laboriously chopped apart the words that had rolled like rainwater off Betsy's tongue. She was so hungry to hear the story again that, exhausted as she was after her thirteen hours in the weaving room, she lay sweating across her bed mouthing in whispers the sounds of Mr. Dickens's narrative.

She was grateful to be alone in the room. There was no one there to make fun of her efforts, or even to try to help. She didn't want help. She didn't want to share this reading with anyone. She was determined to learn the book so well that she would be able to read it aloud to Charlie someday. And wouldn't he be surprised? His Lyddie a real scholar? He'd be monstrous proud.

During the day at the looms, she went over in her head the bits of the story that she had puzzled out the night before. Then it occurred to her that she could copy out pages and paste them up and practice reading them whenever she had a pause. There were not a lot of pauses when she had three machines to tend, so she pasted the copied page on the frame of one of the looms where she could snatch a glance at it as she worked.

July was halfway gone when she made her momentous decision. One fair evening as soon as supper was done, she dressed in her calico, which was nicer than her light summer cotton, put on her bonnet and good boots, and went out on the street. She was trembling when she got to the door of the shop, but she pushed it open. A little bell rang as she did so, and a gentleman who was seated on a high stool behind a slanting desktop looked up at her over his spectacles. "How may I help you, miss?" he asked politely.

She tried to control the shaking in her voice, but in the end was unable to. "I—I come to purchase the book," she said.

The gentleman slid off his stool and waited for her to continue. But Lyddie had already made her rehearsed speech. She didn't have any more words prepared. Finally, he leaned toward her and said in the kindliest sort of voice, "What book did you have in mind, my dear?"

How stupid she must seem to him! The shop was nothing but shelves and shelves of books, hundreds, perhaps thousands of books. "Uh-uh *Oliver Twist*, if you please, sir," she managed to stammer out.

"Ah," he said. "Mr. Dickens. An admirable choice."

He showed her several editions, some rudely printed on cheap paper with only paper backing, but there was only one she wanted. It was beautifully bound in leather with gold letters stamped on its spine. It would take all her money, she knew. Maybe it would be more than she had. She looked fearfully at the kind clerk.

"That will be two dollars," he said. "Shall I wrap it for you?"

She handed him two silver dollars from her purse. "Yes," she said, sighing with relief, "Yes, thank you, sir." And clutching her treasure, she ran from the shop and would have run all the way back to the boardinghouse except that she realized that people on the street were turning to stare.

The Sundays of July were too precious to think of going to church. She didn't even go to the big Sunday School Union picnic on the Fourth, though the sound of the fireworks sent her running from her room to the kitchen. There was no one at home to explain the fearsome racket, but she satisfied herself that the iron cook stove had not blown up, and returned to her sweltering bedroom to continue reading and copying. Mrs. Bedlow gave a general reminder at breakfast on the third Sabbath that many of her boarders were neglecting divine worship, and that the corporation would be most vexed if attendance did not soon improve among the inhabitants of Number Five.

Lyddie slipped a copied page of her book into her pocket and managed to read through the long Methodist sermon. In this way, she only lost a little study time during the two-hour service. She was startled once into attention during the Scripture reading. "Why do you, a Jew, ask water of me a Samaritan?" the woman asked Jesus in the Gospel story. Jesus a Jew? Just like the wicked Fagin? No one had ever told her that Jesus was a Jew before. Just like Fagin, and yet not like Fagin at all.

Lyddie studied on it as she walked home after the service. "Will you watch where you're going, please." She had walked straight into a stout woman in her Sunday best. Lyddie murmured an apology, but the woman humphed angrily and readjusted her bonnet, mumbling something under her breath that ended in "factory girls."

The sidewalk was too crowded for daydreaming. Lyddie packed her wonderings away in her head to think about some other time and began to watch where she was going.

It was then that she saw Diana, or thought she did. At any rate she saw a couple, a handsome, bearded gentleman with a well-dressed lady on his arm, walking toward her on the opposite side of Merrimack Street. The woman was Diana, Lyddie was sure of it. Without thinking, Lyddie called out to her.

But the woman turned her head away. Perhaps she was embarrassed to have a girl yelling rudely at her across a public thoroughfare. Then several carriages and a cart rolled past them, and before Lyddie could see them again, the man and woman had disappeared into the crowd of Sunday strollers. She must have been mistaken. Diana would have recognized her and come across to speak.

12

I Will Not Be
a Slave

She was good at her work—fast, nimble-fingered, diligent, and even in the nearly unbearable heat of the weaving room, apparently indefatigable. The overseer noticed from his high corner stool. Lyddie saw him watching, and she could tell by the smile on his little round lips that he was pleased with her. One afternoon a pair of foreign dignitaries toured the mill, and Mr. Marsden brought them over to watch Lyddie work. She tried to smile politely, but she felt like a prize sow at a village auction.

They didn't pause long. One of them spent the whole time mopping his face and neck and muttering foreign phrases which Lyddie was sure had to do with the temperature rather than the marvels of the Concord Corporation. The other stood by blinking the perspiration from his eyes, looking as though he might faint at any moment. "One of our best girls," Mr. Marsden said, beaming. "One of our very best."

The pay reflected her proficiency. She was making almost $2.50 a week above her $1.75 board. While the other girls grumbled that their piece rates had dropped so that it had hardly been worth slaving through the summer heat, she kept her silence. With Diana gone, she had no friends in the weaving room. She worked too hard to waste precious time getting a drink at the water bucket or running out to the staircase to snatch a breath of air. Besides, her *Oliver* was pasted up, and any free moment her eyes went to the text. She read and reread the page for the day until she nearly had the words by heart.

In this way, she found that even the words that had seemed impossible to decipher on first reading began to make sense as she discovered their place in the story. The names, though peculiar, were the easiest because she remembered them well from Betsy's reading. She liked the names—Mr. Bumble, a villain, but, like her bear, a clumsy one. You had to laugh at his attempts to be somebody in a world that obviously despised him.

Bill Sikes—a name like a rapier—a real villain with nothing to dilute the evil of him, not even Nancy's love. She did not ask herself how a woman could stay with a man like Sikes. Even in her short life she had known of women who clung to fearsome husbands.

Fagin she understood a bit. If the world despised you so much, you were apt to seek revenge on it. The boy thieves—what choice did they have with no homes or families—only workhouses that pretended Christian charity and dealt out despair?

She knew with a shudder how close the family had come to being on the mercy of the town that winter her mother had fled with the babies. Was it to save them from the poor farm that she had gone? Lyddie had not thought of it that way before. Her mother might have realized that she and Charlie on their own were stout enough to manage, but with the extra burden of their mother and the babies . . . Had their mother really thought the bear was the devil on earth? Had she really thought the end was near? Lyddie wondered if she'd ever know the truth of that, anymore than she would ever know what had become of their father.

A letter came to Number Five in her mother's handwriting.

Lyddie felt a pang as she ran to fetch the coins to reimburse Mrs. Bedlow for the postage. She hadn't yet sent any money to her mother. She'd been meaning to. She even had a few dollars set aside for the purpose, but her head had been tied up in other things—her work, the boardinghouse, the dream world of a book—and she had neglected the poor who were her own flesh.

She wanted not to have to open the letter. She wanted the letter never to have arrived, but there it was, and it had to be faced.

Dear Datter,

I was exceding surpriz to get your letter consern yr mov to Lowell. I do not no to say. if you can send muny it will be help to Judah and Clarissa. They fel a grate burdun. Babby Agnes is gone to God. Rachel is porely. Miny hav died, but Gods will be dun.

Yr. loving mother,
Mattie M. Worthen

She tried to remember Agnes's little face. She strained, squenching her eyes tight to get a picture of her sister, now gone forever. She was a baby. She couldn't have been more than four the winter of the bear, but that was now nearly two years past. She would have changed. Maybe she didn't even remember me, Lyddie thought. Could she have forgotten me and Charlie? Me, Lyddie, who washed and fed her and dear Charlie who made her laugh? She wanted to cry but no tears came, only a hard, dry knot in the place where her heart should have been.

She must work harder. She must earn all the money to pay what they owed, so she could gather her family together back on the farm while she still had family left to gather. The idea of living alone and orphaned and without brother or sister—a life barren of land and family like Diana's . . .

So it was that when the Concord Corporation once again speeded up the machinery, she, almost alone, did not complain. She only had two looms to tend instead of the four she'd tended during the summer. She needed the money. She had to have the money. Some of the girls had no sooner come back from their summer holidays than they went home again. They could not keep up the pace. Lyddie was given another loom and then another, and even at the increased speed of each loom, she could tend all four and felt a satisfying disdain for those who could not do the work.

Prudence was the first of the roommates to go home for good. The suitor in Rutland was urging her to give up factory life, but there was a more compelling reason for her to return. She had begun coughing, a dry, painful cough through the night that kept both Betsy and Amelia awake, though not Lyddie. She slept like a caterpillar in winter. Indeed, she was cocooned from all the rest. Betsy had not offered to read another novel to Lyddie since the summer. She and several other operatives had formed study groups, one in Latin and another in botany. On Tuesday and Thursday evenings they commandeered half the parlor of Number Five and hired their own teacher. When Betsy wasn't downstairs with her group, she was in the room preparing for her next session. "Would you like me to read the text to you?" she asked Lyddie once, taking her nose out from between the pages of her botany book.

Lyddie smiled and shook her head. She knew about plants and flowers, at least as much as she craved to know. She didn't know enough about Oliver Twist.

With Prudence gone and the parlor congested, Amelia was often in the room. She insisted on talking, though Betsy, when there, ignored her and Lyddie tried hard to.

"The two of you should be exercising your bodies instead of holing up in this stuffy room reading," Amelia said.

No answer.

"Or at the least, stretching your souls."

No reply, though both Lyddie and Betsy knew that Amelia was reminding them that it was the Sabbath and neither of them had gone to services earlier.

"What are you reading, Lyddie?"

Maybe if I pretend not to hear, she'll leave me be.

"Lyddie!" This time she spoke so sharply that Lyddie looked up, startled. "Get your nose out of that book and come take a walk with me. We won't have many more lovely Sunday afternoons like this. It will be getting cold soon."

"I'm busy," Lyddie mumbled.

Amelia came closer. "You've been reading that same book for months." She reached over and took *Oliver Twist* out of Lyddie's hands.

"That's my book, ey!"

"Come on, Lyddie. Just a short walk by the river before supper. It will do you good."

'Will you get her out of here before I gag her with my bonnet ribbons and lash her to the bedpost?" Betsy said tightly, never taking her eyes off her own book.

"She can walk by herself. I got to read my book." Lyddie stretched her hand to take the book back, but Amelia held it up just out of reach.

"Oh, come," she said. "You've already read this book. I've seen you, and besides, it's only a silly novel—not fit for reading, and a sin on the Sabbath—"

Lyddie could feel the gorge rising in her throat. Silly novel? It was life and death. "You ain't read it," she said, forgetting her grammar in her anger. "How can you know?"

Amelia flushed and her eyes blinked rapidly. She was no longer teasing. "I know about novels," she said, her voice high and a little shaky. "They are the devil's instrument to draw impressionable young minds to perdition."

Lyddie stared at Amelia with her mouth wide open.

It was Betsy who spoke. "For pity's sake, Amelia. Where did you ever hear such pompous nonsense?"

Amelia's face grew redder "You are unbelievers and scoffers, and I don't see how I can continue to live in the same room with you."

"Oh, hush." Betsy's tones were gentler than her words. "We do you no harm. Can't we just live and let live?"

Amelia began to cry. Her chiseled marble features crumbled into the angry, helpless rage of a child. As Lyddie watched, she could feel the hardness inside herself breaking, like jagged cracks across granite.

She got a clean handkerchief from her own box and handed it to the older girl. "Here," she said.

Amelia glanced quickly at the hanky—making sure it was a clean one, Lyddie thought wryly—but she murmured a thank you and blew her nose. "I don't know what possessed me," she said, more in her old tone.

"We're all working like black slaves, is what," said Betsy. "I've half a mind to sign the blooming petition."

"Oh Betsy, you wouldn't!" Amelia lifted her nose out of the handkerchief, her eyes wide.

"Wouldn't I just? When I started in the spinning room, I could do a thirteen-hour day and to spare. But in those days I had a hundred thirty spindles to tend. Now I've twice that many at a speed that would make the devil curse. I'm worn out, Amelia. We're all worn out."

"But we'd be paid less." Couldn't Betsy understand that? "If we just work ten hours, we'd be paid much less."

"Time is more precious than money, Lyddie girl. If only I had two more free hours of an evening—what I couldn't do."

"Should you sign the petition, Betsy, they'll dismiss you. I know they will." Amelia folded the handkerchief and handed it back to Lyddie with a nod.

"And would you miss me, Amelia? I thought you'd consider

it good riddance. I thought I was the blister on your heel these last four years."

"I'm thinking of you. What will you do with no job? You'd be blacklisted. No other corporation would hire you."

"Oh," said Betsy, "maybe I'd just take off West. I've nearly the money." She smiled slyly at Lyddie. "I'm thinking of going out to Ohio."

"Ohio?"

"Hurrah!" Betsy cried out. "That's it! I wait till I've got all the money I need, sign the petition, and exit this city of spindles in a veritable fireworks of defiance."

"No!" Lyddie was startled herself that she had spoken so sharply. Both girls looked at her. "I mean, please, don't sign. I can't. I got to have the money. I got to pay the debts before—"

"Oh Lyddie, hasn't your friend Diana explained it all to you? We're working longer hours, tending more machines, all of which have been speeded to demon pace, so the corporation can make a packet of money. Our real wages have gone down more often than they've gone up. Merciful heaven! Why waste our time on a paper petition? Why not a good old-fashioned turnout?" Betsy put her botany book on the counterpane face down to save the place, hugged her knees, and began to sing in a high childlike soprano:

"Oh! Isn't it a pity such a pretty girl as I
Should be sent to the factory to pine away and
    die?
Oh! I cannot be a slave,
I will not be a slave,
For I'm so fond of liberty
That I cannot be a slave."

"I ain't a slave!" said Lyddie fiercely. "I ain't a slave."

"Of course you aren't." Amelia's confidence had returned and with it her schoolmarm manner.

"At the inn I worked sometimes fifteen, sixteen hours a day and they paid my mother fifty cents a week, if they remembered. Here—"

"Oh shush, girl. Nobody's calling you a slave. I was just singing the old song."

"How do you know that radical song?" Amelia asked.

"I was a doffer back in '36. At ten you learn all the songs."

"And did you join the turnout?" Now Amelia looked like a schoolmarm who had caught a child in mischief.

Betsy's eyes blazed. "At ten? I led out my whole floor— running all the way. It was the most exciting day of my life!"

"It does no good to rebel against authority."

"Well, it does me good. I'm sick of being a sniveling wage slave." Betsy picked up her botany book again as though closing the discussion.

"I mean it's . . . it's unladylike and . . . and against the Scriptures." Amelia's voice was shaking as she spoke.

"Against the Bible to fight injustice? Oh, come now, Amelia. I think you've got the wrong book at that church of yours."

Lyddie looked from one angry face to the other. She cared nothing for being a lady or being religious. She was making far more money than she ever had at home in Vermont or was ever likely to. Why couldn't people just live and let live?

The clang of the curfew bell quieted the argument but not Lyddie's anxiety.

13
Speed Up

Lyddie could not keep the silly song out of her head. It clacked and whistled along with the machinery.

> Oh! I cannot be a slave,
> I will not be a slave . . .

She *wasn't* a slave. She was a free woman of the state of Vermont, earning her own way in the world. Whatever Diana, or even Betsy, might think, she, Lyddie, was far less a slave than most any girl she knew of. They mustn't spoil it for her with their petitions and turnouts. They mustn't meddle with the system and bring it all clanging down to ruin.

She liked Diana, really she did, yet she found herself avoiding her friend as though radicalism were something catching, like diptheria. She knew Mr. Marsden was beginning to keep track of the girls who stopped by Diana's looms. She could see him watching and taking mental note.

When Diana came her way, Lyddie could feel herself stiffening up. And when Diana invited her to one of the Tuesday night meetings, Lyddie said *"No!"* so fiercely that she scared herself. Diana didn't ask again. It ain't about you, Lyddie wanted to say. It's me. I just want to go home. Please understand, Diana, it ain't about you.

The ten-hour people were putting out a weekly newspaper,

The Voice of Industry. Lyddie tried to keep her eyes from straying toward the copies of the weekly, which were thrown with seeming carelessness on the parlor table. Then one night after supper she and Amelia came upstairs to find Betsy chortling over the paper in their bedroom.

"Here!" she said, holding it out to Lyddie. "Read this! Those plucky women are going after the legislature now!"

Lyddie recoiled as though someone had offered her the hot end of a poker.

"Oh Lyddie," Betsy said. "Don't be afraid to read something you might not agree with."

"Leave Lyddie alone, Betsy. You'll only get her into trouble."

"Never fret, Amelia. Our Lyddie loves money too much to risk trouble."

Lyddie flushed furiously. She *was* worried about the money, but she wished Betsy wouldn't put it like that. She wanted to explain to them—to justify herself. Maybe if she told them about the bear—about how close her family'd come to moving to the poor farm. Maybe if she told them about Charlie—how bright he was and how she knew he could do as good at college as Betsy's stuckup brother. Only Charlie wasn't at Harvard. He was sweeping chaff off a mill floor. And little Agnes had gone to God. She shuddered and held her peace. It might sound like cowardly excuses when the words were formed. But it didn't matter if they understood or not. As much as she admired Diana, she wouldn't be tricked by her, or even by Betsy, to joining any protest. Just another year or two and she could go home—home free. I got to write Mama, she thought. I got to tell her how hard I'm working to pay off the debt.

Dear Mother,
    I was made quite sad by your letter telling of my sister Agnes's death. I am consern that you are not taking proper

care of your health. I have enclose one dollar. Please get yourself and little Rachel good food and if possible a warm shawl for the winter. I will send more next payday. I try to save for the debt, but you must tell me how much it is exakly. And do I send it direct to Mr. Wescott or to some bank? I am well. I work hard.

> Your loving daughter,
> Lydia Worthen

She checked her spelling in *Oliver*. The grammar as well. She felt a little thrill of pride. She knew she was improving in her writing. Not that her mother would be able to tell, but Charlie would. She took a second sheet to begin a letter to him, then hesitated, suddenly shy. It had been so long. She hardly knew what to say. I must go to see him soon as my year is up, she thought. I'll lose touch. Or—he'll forget me. She jerked her head to loosen the thought. Charlie would no more forget her than the snow would forget to fall on Camel's Hump Mountain. But she should write. He might think she had forgotten him.

Dear Charlie,

No, "Dear Charles." (He was nearly a man now and might not like a pet name.)

Dear Charles,

She held the pen so tight her fingers cramped.

> I have heard from Mother that little Agnes has died. Did she write you as well this sad news? We must get Mother and Rachel home soon. I am saving most of my wages for the debt. I am working hard and making good pay. We can go home soon I stil hop. (ha ha). I trust you are well.
>
> I am as ever your loving sister,
> Lydia Worthen

A great blob of ink fell from the pen right at her name. She blotted it, but the black spread up into the body of the letter. She tried to tell herself that it didn't matter—that Charlie would not be bothered, but she was too bothered by it herself. She'd meant the letter to show him how well she was doing—how she was learning and studying as well as working, but the black stain ruined it. She destroyed the page and could not seem to start another.

No matter how fast the machines speeded up, Lyddie was somehow able to keep pace. She never wasted energy worrying or complaining. It was almost as if they had exchanged natures, as though she had become the machine, perfectly tuned to the roaring, clattering beasts in her care. Think of them as bears she'd tell herself. Great, clumsy bears. You can face down bears.

From his high stool at the back corner of the great room, she could almost feel the eyes of the overseer upon her. Indeed, when Mr. Marsden got up to stroll the room he always stopped at her looms. She was often startled by the touch of his puffy white hand upon her sleeve, and when she turned, his little mouth would be forming something she took to be complimentary, for his eyes were crinkled as though the skin about them had cracked in the attempt to smile.

She would nod acknowledgment and turn back to her machines, which at least did not reach out and pat you when you weren't watching.

He was a strange little man. Lyddie tried once to imagine him dressing in the morning. His impeccable wife tying that impeccable tie, brushing down that black coat, which by six A.M. would be white with the lint blowing about the gigantic room. Did she polish his head as well? And with what? You couldn't use shoeblack of course. Was there a head grease that could be applied and then rubbed to a high shine? She saw the overseer's impeccable wife with the end of a towel in either hand briskly polishing her husband's head, just above the ears, then carefully combing back the few strands of grayish hair from one ear to the other. It was hard to put a face on the overseer's wife. Was she a meek, obedient little woman, or someone like Mrs. Cutler, who would rule him as he ruled the girls under his watchful eye? Not a happy woman, though, for Mr. Marsden did not seem to be the stuff from which contentment could be woven.

Soon there was little time to wonder and daydream. She had done so well on her two, then three, machines that Mr. Marsden gave her a fourth loom to tend. Now she hardly noticed people anymore. At mealtimes the noise and complaints and banter of the other girls were like the commotion of a distant parade. She paid no attention that the food was not as bountiful as it had once been. There was still more than she could eat. Nor did she notice that the taste of the meat was a bit off or the potatoes moldy. She ate the food set before her steadily, with no attempt to bolt as much as possible in the short time allotted. When the bell rang, it didn't matter what was left untasted, she simply pushed back from the table and went back to her bears.

She was too tired now at night to copy out a page of *Oliver* to paste to her loom. It hardly mattered. When would she have had time to study it? After supper she stumbled upstairs, hardly taking time to wash, changed to her shift, and fell into bed.

Though Amelia cajoled and Mrs. Bedlow made announcements at mealtime, Lyddie did not attempt to go to church. Her body wouldn't have cooperated even if she'd had the desire to go. She slept out Sunday mornings and forced herself up for dinner, which she ate, as she ate all her meals now, automatically and without conversation. She was as likely to nap again in the afternoon as not.

"It's like being a racehorse," Betsy was saying. "The harder we work, the bigger prize they get."

Amelia murmured something in reply, which Lyddie was too near sleep to make out.

"I've made up my mind to sign the next petition."

"You wouldn't!"

"Wouldn't I just?" Betsy laughed. "The golden lad finishes Harvard this spring. His fees are paid up, and I've got nearly the money I need now. My Latin is done. So as soon as I complete my botany course, I'll be ready to leave this insane asylum."

Even Lyddie's sleep-drugged mind could feel a twinge. She did not want Betsy to go.

"It would be grand—going out with the bang of a dishonorable dismissal."

"But where would you go? You've always said you could never settle in Maine."

"Not to Maine, Amelia. To Ohio. I'm aiming to go to college."

"To college?"

"Do I surprise you, Amelia? Betsy, in public the devourer of novels, in secret a woman of great ambition?"

"College. I wouldn't have imagined—"

"If they dismiss me, I'd have to stop stalling and blathering and get myself to Oberlin College and a new life." By now, Lyddie was propped up on her elbow listening, torn between pride for Betsy and horror at what she was proposing. "So, you're awake after all, our sleeping beauty."

"Lyddie, tell her not to be foolish."

"I'd hate you to leave," Lyddie said quietly.

Betsy snorted. "I'd be gone a month and a half before you'd ever notice," she said.

The overseers were being offered premiums—prizes to the men whose girls produced the most goods in a pay period—

which was why the machines were speeded and why the girls hardly dared take time off even when they were feverish.

"If you can't do the work," Lyddie heard Mr. Marsden say to a girl at the breakfast break, "there's many a girl who can and will. We've no place for sickly girls in this room."

Many girls—those with families who could support them or sweethearts ready to marry them—went home, and new girls came in to replace them. Their speech was strange and their clothing even stranger. They didn't live in the corporation boardinghouses but in that part of the city known as "the Acre."

The Acre wasn't part of the tour for foreign dignitaries who came to view the splendor of Lowell—the model factory city of the New World. Near the Northern Canal, sprouting up like toadstools, rose the squat shacks of rough boards and turf with only a tiny window and a few holes to let in light. And each jammed with Irish Catholics who, it was said, bred like wharf rats. Rumor also had it that these papists were willing to work for lower wages, and, since the corporations did not subsidize their board and keep, the Irish girls were cheaper still to hire.

Diana was helping the new girls settle in, teaching them just as she had taught Lyddie in the spring. Lyddie herself was far too busy to help anyone else. She could not fall behind in her production, else her pay would drop and before she knew it one of these cussed papists would have her job.

Often, now, the tune came unbidden to her head:

> Oh! I cannot be a slave,
> I will not be a slave . . .

It was a dreary December without the abundance of snow that Lyddie yearned for. What snow fell soon turned to a filthy sludge under the feet of too many people and the soot and ashes from too many chimneys. Her body itched even more than it usually did in winter. The tub of hot water, that first night in Mrs. Bedlow's bedroom, proved to be her only full bath in the city, for, like most of the companies, the Concord Corporation had not seen fit to provide bathhouses for their workers. The girls were obliged to wash themselves using only the wash basins in their rooms, to which Tim hauled a pitcher of cold water once a day.

Despite the winter temperatures, the factory stayed hot with the heat of the machinery, the hundreds of whale oil lamps lit against the winter's short, dark days, and the steam piped into the rooms to keep the air humid lest warp threads break needlessly and precious time and materials be wasted.

Lyddie went to work in the icy darkness and returned again at night. She never saw the sun. The brief noon break did not help. The sky was always oppressive and gray, and the smoke of thousands of chimneys hung low and menacing.

At the Lawrence Corporation, just down the riverbank from the Concord, a girl had slipped on the icy staircase in the rush to dinner. She had broken her neck in the fall. And the very same day, a man loading finished bolts of cloth onto the railroad cars in the Lawrence mill yard had been run over and crushed. There were no deaths at the Concord Corporation, but one of the little Irish girls in the spinning room had caught her hair in the machinery and was badly hurt.

Diana took up a collection for the hospital fees, but Lyddie had no money on her person. Besides, how could she give a contribution to some foreigner when she had her own poor baby sister to think of? She vowed to send her mother something next payday. She had opened a bank account and it was growing. She watched it the way one watched a heifer, hardly patient for the time to come when you could milk it. She tried not to resent withdrawing money to send to her mother, but she could see the balance grow each payday. She hadn't seen her mother for two years. She had no way of knowing what her true needs were. And surely, as mean as Judah was and as crazy as Clarissa might be, they would not let their own sister or her child go hungry.

Christmas was not a holiday. It came and went hardly noticed. Amelia had a New Year's gift from her mother—a pair of woolen gloves, which she wrapped again in the paper they had come in and hid in her trunk. Only someone fresh from the farm or one of the Irish would wear a pair of homemade gloves in Lowell. Betsy's brother sent her a volume of essays "to improve my mind." She laughed about his gift, knowing that it had been bought out of the money she sent him each month for his school allowance. "Oh, well," she said. "Only a few more months and our golden lad will be on his own. Ah, if only our sexes had been reversed! Imagine him putting *me* through college."

Lyddie received no gifts, indeed expected none, but she did get a note from Triphena, who thanked her for returning the loan. There was little news to report from Cutler's. She asked after Lyddie's health and complained that the mistress was as harsh as ever. Willie had run off at last, and the new boy and girl weren't worth two blasts on a penny whistle. Lyddie had to smile. Poor Triphena.

Was she thinking of Triphena when it happened? Or was she overtired? It was late on Friday—the hardest time of the week. Was she careless when she replaced the shuttle in the right-hand box or had there been a knot in the weft thread? She would never know. She remembered rethreading the shuttle and putting it back in the race, yanking the lever into its slot . . . Before she could think she was on the floor, blood pouring through the hair near her right temple . . . the shuttle, the blasted shuttle. She tried to rise, she needed to stop the loom, but Diana got there almost at once, racing along the row, tripping with both hands the levers of her own machines and Lyddie's four as she ran. She knelt down beside Lyddie.

"Dear God," she said, cradling Lyddie's head in her lap. She pulled her handkerchief from her pocket and held it tight against Lyddie's temple. It filled immediately with blood. She eased her apron out from under Lyddie's head, snatched it off her shoulders, and pressed it against the soaked handkerchief.

Girls had begun to gather. "Get me some cold water, Delia— clean!" she cried after the girl. "And handkerchiefs, please. All of you!" she cried to the girls crowding about them.

Mr. Marsden's head appeared in the circle of heads above them. The girls shifted to make room for the overseer. "What's this here?" His voice was stern, but his face went ashen as he looked down at the two girls.

"She was hit by the shuttle," Diana said.

"What?" he yelled above the noise.

"Shuttle—shuttle—shuttle." The word whished back and forth across the circle like a shuttle in a race.

"Well . . . well . . . get her out of here." He clamped a large blue pocket handkerchief over his nose and mouth and hurried back to his high stool.

"Not partial to the sight of blood, are we?" The speaker was kneeling on the floor beside Diana, offering her the dainty white handkerchiefs she had collected from the operatives.

The cool water came at last. Diana lifted her apron from Lyddie's temple. The first gush of blood had eased now to a trickle. She dipped a handkerchief into the water and, gently as a cow licking its newborn, cleaned the wound. "Can you see all right?" she asked.

"I think so." Lyddie's head pounded, but when she opened her eyes she could see nearly as well as she ever could in the dusty, lamp-lit room. She closed her eyes almost at once against the pain.

"How about your stomach? Do you feel sick?" Lyddie shook her head, then stopped. Any movement seemed to make the pain worse.

There was a sound of ripping cloth at Lyddie's ear. She opened her eyes. "Your apron," Lyddie said. "Don't—" Aprons cost money.

Diana seemed not to hear, continuing to tear until her apron was in shreds. She bound the least bloodied pieces around Lyddie's head and tied them in place with a narrower strip. "Do you think you could stand up?" she asked.

In answer, Lyddie started to get up. Diana and Delia helped her to her feet. "Just stand here for a minute," Diana said. "Don't try to move yet."

The room spun. She reached out toward the beam of the loom to steady herself. Diana put her arm around Lyddie's shoulders. "Lean on me," she said. "I'll take you home."

"The bell ain't rung," Lyddie protested weakly.

"Oh Lyddie, Lyddie," Diana said, "whatever shall we do with you?" She sighed and pulled Lyddie close. "Delia, help us down the stairs, please. I think I can get her the rest of the way by myself."

Slowly, slowly they went, stopping every few feet to rest. "We don't want to open that cut again," Diana said. "Easy, easy." Mrs. Bedlow helped Diana take Lyddie up the stairs to the second-floor infirmary, not her own room as she wished. But Lyddie's head pounded too much for her to insist that they take her up still another flight of stairs.

"I'll send Tim for Dr. Morris," she heard Mrs. Bedlow saying. No, no, Lyddie wanted to say. Doctors cost money.

"No," Diana was saying. "Not Dr. Morris. Dr. Craven. On Fletcher Street."

She was asleep when the doctor arrived, but she opened her eyes when she heard the murmur of voices above her. "Lyddie," Diana was saying softly, "Dr. Craven needs to look at the wound."

They were there, the two of them standing above her, Diana's familiar face flushed, smiling anxiously down at her, and the doctor's . . . He was a handsome, bearded gentleman—young, his dark brown eyes studying her own, his long, thin hands already reaching to loosen Diana's makeshift bandage. "Now let's look at that cut of yours," he said in a tone compounded of concern and assurance—the perfect doctor.

Lyddie gasped.

He drew his hands back. "Are you in pain?" he asked.

Lyddie shook her head. It was not pain that had startled her. It was the doctor himself. She had seen him before—with Diana—last summer on Merrimack Street.

14

Ills and Petitions

By Saturday afternoon she was back in her own room, and by Sunday the pain had dulled. Dr. Craven had cut her hair away from the wound and bound her head in a proper bandage, but she took it off. She was going back to work the next day, bald spot and all. She'd never been vain—never had anything to be vain about, to tell the truth. No need to start in fussing over her looks now.

At first Amelia and Mrs. Bedlow objected to her returning to work so soon, but they quickly gave up. Lyddie would go to work no matter what. "If you can't do the work . . . ," Mr. Marsden had said. Besides, Diana came by Sunday evening and said she was looking quite fit again. Diana should know, shouldn't she?

She went to bed early, but she couldn't sleep. Her head seemed to throb more when she was lying down. She thought about her family—suppose that cussed shuttle had killed her, or put out her eye? What would they do? And Diana. What was Lyddie to think? She hadn't dared ask about Dr. Craven. Diana hadn't explained why she sent for him instead of Dr. Morris, who usually cared for the girls at Number Five. Dr. Craven seemed as good a doctor as any—better. He didn't leave a bill.

The curfew bell rang. Amelia came to bed. Betsy did too,

though she kept her candle burning, studying into the night as she often did. At last she blew out the light, and slid down under the quilts. Then it began, that awful tearing sound that Lyddie would come to dread with every knotted inch of nerves through her whole silently screeching body. Finally it stopped.

"Betsy, I *do* wish you'd see Dr. Morris about that cough." Amelia's voice came from the next bed.

"I'm a big girl, Amelia. Don't nag."

"I'm not nagging. If you weren't so stubborn . . ."

"What would he tell me, Amelia? To rest? How can I do that? I've only got a few more months to go. If I stop now—"

"*I'm* going to stop."

"What?"

There was a sigh in the darkness. "I'm leaving—going home."

"Home?"

"I—I've come to hate factory life. Oh Betsy, I hate what it's doing to me. I don't even know myself anymore. This corporation is turning me into a sour old spinster."

"It's just the winter." Betsy's voice was kinder than usual. "It's hard to stay cheerful in the dark. Come spring you'll be our resident saint once more."

Amelia ignored the tease. "I've been through winter before," she said. "It's not the season." She sighed again, more deeply than before. "I'm tired, Betsy. I can't keep up the pace."

"Who can? Except our Amazonian Lyddie?" Betsy's laugh turned abruptly into a cough that shook the whole bed.

Lyddie scrunched up tightly into herself and tried to block out the sound and the rusty saw hacking through her own chest. Had Betsy been coughing like this for long? Why hadn't she heard it before? Surely there must be some syrup or tonic, even opium . . .

"You *must* see the doctor about that cough," Amelia said. "Promise me you will."

"I'll make a pact with you, Amelia. I'll see the doctor if you'll promise to stay until summer. I can't think of Number Five without you." She stopped to cough, then cleared her throat and said in a still husky voice, "How could I manage? You're the plague of my life—my—my guardian angel."

There was a funny kind of closeness between her roommates after that night, but even so, Amelia went home the last week of January to visit and didn't come back. She wrote that her father had found her a teaching post in the next village. "Forgive me, Betsy," she wrote. "And do, please, I beg you, go to see the doctor."

With a bed to herself, Lyddie was less distressed by Betsy's coughing. And though Betsy never quite got around to seeing Dr. Morris, she was better, Lyddie told herself. Surely the cough was less wracking than it had been. Lyddie missed Amelia. She would have imagined that she'd feel relief to have her gone, but Betsy was right. They both needed her in an odd sort of way—their nettlesome guardian angel.

Her cut was quite healed. Her hair grew out and covered the scar. She was working as well and as hard as ever. Her January pay came to eleven dollars and twenty cents, exclusive of board. Everything was going well for her when Mr. Marsden stopped her one evening as she was about to leave. The machines were quiet, so she could not pretend deafness.

"You're feeling fine again? No problems with the—the head?" She nodded and made as if to go. "You have to take care of yourself. You're my best girl, you know." He put his hand on her sleeve. She looked down at it, and he slipped it off. His face reddened slightly, and his little round mouth worked a bit on the next sentence.

"We're getting new operators in tomorrow—not nearly so

clever as you, but promising. If I could put one in your care—let her work as a spare hand on one of your machines."

Oh, hang it all. How could she say no? How could she explain that she must not be slowed down? She couldn't have some dummy monkeying with her looms. "I got to make my pieces," she muttered.

"Yes," he said, "of course you do. It would only be for a day or so. I wouldn't let anyone hinder you." He smiled with his mouth and not his eyes. "You're my prize girl here."

I'm not your girl. I'm not anybody's girl but my own.

"So—it's settled," he said, reaching out as though to pat her again, but Lyddie quickly shifted her arm to escape the touch.

The new girl, Brigid, was from the Acre—an Irish papist through and through, wearing layers of strange capes and smelling even worse than Lyddie herself. Lyddie scented more than poverty and winter sweat. She whiffed disaster. The girl's only asset was a better command of proper New England speech than most of her lot. Not that she spoke often. She seemed deafened by the machinery and too cowed to ask questions even when she needed to.

As for tying knots, a basic weaver's knot, the girl simply couldn't do them. Lyddie demonstrated—her powdered fingers pinching, looping, slipping, pulling—all in one fluid motion that magically produced a healed warp thread with no hint of a lump to betray the break.

"You don't even watch!" the girl cried out in alarm. And, of course, Lyddie didn't. She had no need to. Her fingers could have tied that knot in a privy at midnight, and it would have held. It would have been invisible as well.

"Here," she said, barely clinging to patience. "I'll do it more slowly." She slapped off all four machines. With her scissors, she cut two threads from a bobbin and, taking the girl to the window where the light was best, she wasted at least five precious minutes tying and retying the useless knot until, finally, the girl was able, however clumsily, to tie a lumpy knot herself.

Lyddie jerked a nod. "It will get better with practice," she said gruffly, anxious to get the stilled looms roaring once more.

Threading the shuttle was, if anything, worse. Lyddie popped the full bobbin into the shuttle and then, as always, put her mouth to the hole and sucked the thread through, pulled it to length, wrapped it quickly on a hook of the temple, dropped the shuttle into the race, and restarted the loom. The next time the quill had to be replaced, she had Brigid thread it, and, as she watched the girl put her mouth over the hole and suck out the thread, the words *kiss of death* came to mind. She had always thought the words a joke among the weavers, but here was this strange-smelling foreigner sucking Lyddie's shuttles, leaving her spittle all over the thread hole. Lyddie wiped the point quickly on her apron before she banged the shuttle against the far end of the race. "We don't want any flying shuttles," she yelled, her face nearly as crimson as the Irish girl's.

By the end of the first day, the girl was far from ready to operate her own machine, but Lyddie had run out of patience. She told Mr. Marsden to assign the girl a loom next to her own. "I'll watch out for her and tend my own machines as well."

Before the noon break of the next day, a flying shuttle had grazed the girl's shoulder, and she had let the shuttle run out of weft, ruining several inches of cloth. When a warp thread snapped, instead of instantly hitting the lever to stall the loom, she threw her apron over her head and burst into tears.

"Shut off your loom," Lyddie yelled over to her. "You can tie the knot this time. You should know how by now, ey?" The girl burst into tears again, and before Lyddie could decide what to do with her, Diana was there, slapping off the loom. Burning with shame, Lyddie glanced over as Diana, without a quiver of impatience, helped the girl retrieve the broken ends and tie a weaver's knot. When, finally, Diana stood back and told the girl to pull the lever into place, Lyddie touched Diana's shoulder. "Sorry," she mouthed.

Diana nodded and went back to work. At the last bell Lyddie found herself going down the stairs beside Diana.

"She's going to do fine, your Brigid," Diana said.

"Oh, I don't know," Lyddie said, wondering how Diana knew the girl's name and then annoyed that the foreigner should be "hers." Surely Lyddie had never wanted her. "She seems all thumbs and tears. They be such fools, those Irish."

Diana gave a wry smile. "We're all allowed to be fools the first week or two, aren't we?"

Lyddie blushed furiously. "I never thanked you proper for taking care of me before," she said. "And your doctor—he never sent a bill. Mind you, I'm not complaining, but—"

Diana didn't comment on the doctor. "Your head seems to have quite recovered. How do you feel? No pain, I hope."

"Oh, I'm all right," Lyddie said. "Just ornery as a old sow."

"Ornery enough to add your name to the petition?" Diana whispered.

She was teasing her, Lyddie was sure of it. "I don't reckon I aim to ever get that ornery," Lyddie said.

Betsy signed the petition. One of the Female Labor Reform girls caught her in an apothecary shop one evening and got her to write in her name.

Lyddie was furious. "They got you when you was feeling low," she said. "They go creeping around the city taking advantage when girls are feeling sick or worn out. Now you'll be blacklisted, and what will I do without you?"

"Better to go out with a flourish than a whine, don't you think?" But Betsy was never allowed her imagined exit. She was to be neither blacklisted nor dismissed.

Her cough got no better. She asked for a transfer to the drawing room. The work of drawing the warp threads from the beam through the harness and reeds had to be done painstakingly by hand. The air was cleaner in the drawing room, and there was much less noise. Though the threading took skill, it did not take the physical strength demanded in the machine rooms, and the girls sat on high stools as they worked. The drawing room was a welcome change for Betsy, but the move came too late to help. The coughing persisted. She began to spend days in their bedroom, then the house infirmary, until, finally, when blood showed up in her phlegm, Mrs. Bedlow demanded that she be removed to the hospital.

On Sunday Lyddie went to see her, taking her botany text and a couple of novels that cost Lyddie twenty cents at the lending library.

"You've got to get me out of here," Betsy said between fits of coughing. "They'll bleed me of every penny I've saved." But where could Betsy go? Mrs. Bedlow would not have her in the house, unwilling to bear the responsibility, and Dr. Morris had declared her too weak to travel to Maine to her uncle's.

Lyddie wrote the brother. He was only in Cambridge—less than a day away by coach or train—but there was a three-week delay before he wrote to say that he was studying for his final examinations and would, perhaps, be able to come for a visit at the end of the term.

Betsy only laughed. "Well," she said, "he's our darling baby boy." Then she fell to coughing. There was a red stain on her handkerchief.

"But you sent him all the way through that college of his."

"Wouldn't you do as much for your Charlie?"

"But Charlie is—" Lyddie was going to say "nice" and stopped herself just in time.

"Our parents are dead, and he's the son and heir," Betsy said as though that explained everything.

Betsy grew a little stronger as the weather warmed, and in April her uncle came to take her to Maine. By then her savings were gone, along with her good looks. "Keep my bed for me, Lyddie. I'll be back next year to start all over again. Someday I'll have enough money to go to college no matter how much the piece rate drops. I may be the oldest girl in the corporation before I have the money again, but if they let women into Oberlin at all, surely they won't fuss about gray hair and a few wrinkles."

She'll never come back, Lyddie thought sadly as she watched the buggy disappear around the corner, headed for the depot and the train north. She'll never be strong enough again to work in a mill thirteen, fourteen hours a day. When I'm ready to go myself, she thought, maybe I could sign that cussed petition. Not for me. I don't need it, but for Betsy and the others. It ain't right for this place to suck the strength of their youth, then cast them off like dry husks to the wind.

He was standing by the front door of Number Five when she came with the rush of girls for the noon meal. "Lyddie Worthen . . ." He said her name so quietly that she almost went past him without hearing. "Miss Lyddie . . ."

She turned toward the voice, which didn't seem familiar, to see a tall man she didn't know. Later she realized that he had not been wearing his broad black Quaker hat. She would have known him at once in his hat. His hair in the sunlight was the rusty red of a robin's breast. Several girls nudged her and giggled as they pushed past her up the steps to the boarding-house.

"I was hoping thee would come," he said. He was so tall he had to stoop over to speak to her. "I'm Luke Stevens." His grave brown eyes searched her face. "Has thee forgotten?"

"No," she said. "I'd not forgot. I just never expected—"

"I wondered if thee would know me in this strange garb." He was wearing shirt and trousers of coarse cotton jean—the kind of cloth the Lowell mills spit out by the mile. She would have known him at once in his Quaker hat and his mother's brown homespun. "I'm fetching some freight from down Boston way," he said almost in a whisper, glancing over his shoulder as he spoke. "They tend to look out for Friends on the road."

"Oh," she said, not really understanding.

"My pa sent thee this," he said, handing her a thick brown parcel about the size of a small book. "He didn't want to risk the post with it, and since I was coming down Boston way—"

She took the parcel from his big, rough farmer fist. "I thank you for your trouble," she said.

"It was no trouble." Was he blushing behind that sun- and wind-weathered face? How odd he seemed.

She felt a need to be polite. "Maybe Mrs. Bedlow could find you some dinner," she said. "We was just coming to eat."

"I can't stay longer. I'm due in Boston. But—but, I'm obliged," he said.

"Well . . ."

"I'd best be on my way . . ."

"Well . . ." She could hear the calls and clatter of the dinner hour even through the closed front door. She'd hardly have a minute to eat her meal if he didn't go.

"It's mighty good to see thee, Lyddie Worthen," he said. "We miss having thee up the hill."

She tried to smile at him. "Thank you for the . . ."—whatever the strange parcel was. "It was good of you to bring it all this way." When on earth would he leave?

"Thy Charlie is well," he said. "I was by the mill just last week."

Charlie. "He's doing well? Fit and—and content?"

"Cheerful as ever. He's a fine boy, Lyddie."

"Yes. I know. Give him my—my best when you see him again, ey?"

He nodded. "Thy house came through the winter in good shape." He saw her glimpse the door. "I mustn't hold thee longer from thy dinner," he said. "God keep you."

"And you," she said.

He grinned good-bye and was gone.

She didn't have time to open the parcel until after supper. Enclosed in several layers of brown paper was a strange, official-looking document, which at first she could make no sense of, and a letter in a strange hand.

My dear Miss Lydia,

By now you have despaired of me and decided that I am a man who does not honor his word. Please forgive my tardiness. Thanks to the good offices of our friends the Stevenses (true Friends, indeed) as well as your gracious loan, I was able to make my way safely to Montreal. I have now the great joy of my family's presence. Enclosed, therefore, herein is a draft which can never repay my great debt to you.

> With everlasting gratitude, your friend,
> Ezekial Freeman

She could not believe it. Fifty dollars. The next day she used her dinner break to race to the bank. Yes, it was a genuine draft from a solvent Montreal bank. Fifty dollars. With one piece of paper her account had bulged like a cow about to freshen. She must find out at once what the debt was. She might already have enough to cover it. Why hadn't her mother replied to her inquiry? Did her mother even know what the debt was? Did she care? Oh mercy, had the woman always hated the farm? Was she glad to have it off her hands?

Lyddie wrote again that very night.

Dear Mother,
   You have not answered my letter of some months prevyus. I need to know the total sum of the det. Writ soon.
                                          Yr. loving daughter,
                                          Lydia Worthen

She didn't take the time to check her spelling. She sealed the letter at once. Then, reluctantly, reopened it to slip in a dollar.

She awoke once in the night and pondered on what she had once been and what she seemed to have become. She marveled that there had been a time when she had almost gladly given a perfect stranger everything she had, but now found it hard to send her own mother a dollar.

15

Rachel

She told no one about the money. She wanted to tell Diana. Diana, she knew, would rejoice with her, but she decided to wait. She was so close now to having the money she needed, and when she did, she would surprise Diana by signing the petition. Then, not more than a week after Luke had brought the money, she had a second visitor who turned her life upside down.

She had left the bedroom door open, trying to encourage a faint breeze through the stuffy room while she washed out her stockings and underwear in the basin. Suddenly she was aware of Tim, standing in the doorway. She looked up from her washing.

"There's a visitor for you in the parlor, Ma says to tell you. A gentleman."

Charlie! She was sure it must be he, all grown up to a gentleman, for who else would come to see her? She could hardly count Luke Stevens. She squeezed the water from her laundry and hastily wiped her hands upon her apron as she ran down the stairs.

But it wasn't Charlie waiting in the corner of the dining room that Mrs. Bedlow called a parlor. Nor was it Luke. She wondered why Tim had called him a "gentleman" at all. At first she was sure he was a stranger. He seemed so out of place in the room of neatly dressed, chattering factory girls, this short man, very thin, with a weathered face and the homespun clothes of a hill farmer.

"Don't you know your uncle, ey?" the man asked at the same moment she recognized him for Judah, Aunt Clarissa's husband, whom she hadn't seen since she was a small thing.

"Made it in two days," he boasted. "Slept right in the wagon."

She tried to smile, but her heart was beating like a churning blade against her breast. What could have brought him here? Anything to do with Clarissa had always spelled trouble. "What's the matter?" She spoke as quietly as she could, feeling every eye in the crowded parlor turned their way. "Why've you come?"

He sobered at once, as though remembering a solemn duty. "Your Aunt Clarissa thought you need be told—"

"Told what?" A chill went through her.

"Your ma's never been stout, you know—"

"The fever? Did she catch the fever?"

He glanced around at the girls seated in the room, who were pretending not to listen, but whose ears stood up, alert as wild creatures in a meadow. He lowered his voice, tapping his head. "Stout up here, ey?"

Lyddie stared at him. What had they done to her mother?

Judah dropped his eyes, uncomfortable under her stare. "So we been obliged—"

"What have you done to my mother?" she whispered fiercely.

"We been obliged to remand her to Brattleboro—to the asylum down there."

"But that's for crazy folk!"

Judah put on a face of hound-dog sorrow and sighed deeply. "It were just too much care for poor Clarissa, delicate as she be."

"Why didn't you ask me? I been responsible for her before. I can do it."

He cocked his head. "You weren't there, ey?"

"Where's Rachel? What have you done with the baby?"

"Why," he said, relieved to have gotten off the subject of her mother, "why she's just fine. Right out front in the wagon. I brung her to you."

Lyddie brushed past him out the door. The farm wagon stood outside; the patient oxen, oblivious to how comically out of place they looked on a city street, chewed their cuds contentedly. For all the stuffiness upstairs, it was damp and chilly down on the street, and Rachel sat shivering on the bench of the wagon, wrapped in a worn shawl that Lyddie recognized as her mother's.

She climbed up on the wagon step and lifted the child down. Rachel was too light. Boneless as a rag doll. As Lyddie went up the steps of the boardinghouse, she could feel her tiny burden trembling through the shawl. "It's all right, Rachie. It's me, Lyddie," she said, hoping the child could remember her.

She carried Rachel inside to where Judah still stood, nervously pinching the rim of his sweat-stained hat. "It's your sister, Rachie," Judah boomed out, his voice fake with hearty cheer. A gasp went up from the girls in the parlor. "Like Aunt Clarissie told you, ey? We brung you to Lyddie."

"Have you got her things?"

In answer he went out to the wagon and brought back a sack with a small lump at the bottom.

"What about my mother's things?" she asked coldly, no longer caring about the audience and what they heard.

"There weren't hardly nothing," he said. She let it go. He was nearly right. "Well," he said, looking from one sister to the other, "I'll be off, then, ey?"

"I'm coming to fetch our mother, soon as I can. As soon

as I pay off the debt. I'll take her back home and care for her myself."

He turned at the door, the hat brim rolled tight and squeezed in his big hands. "Back where?"

"Home," she repeated. "To the farm."

"We be selling it," he said, "We got to have the money—for—for Brattleboro."

"No!" Her voice was so sharp that the roomful of girls stopped everything they were doing to stare. Even little Rachel twisted in her arms to look at her with alarm. She went close to Judah and lowered her voice again to a fierce whisper. "No one can sell that land except my father."

"He give permission."

"How?" She was seized with a wild hope. Her father! They had heard from him. "When?"

"Before he left. He had it wrote out and put his mark to it. In case—ey?"

She wanted to scream at him, but how could she? She had already frightened Rachel. "You got no right," she said between her teeth.

"We got no choice," the man said stubbornly. "We be responsible." And he was gone.

Once more Lyddie was aware of the other girls in the room, who were watching her openmouthed and gaping at the dirty little bundle in her arms. She buried her face in the shawl. "Come on, Rachie," she said as much to them as to the child, "we got to go meet Mrs. Bedlow." She straightened up tall and made her way through the chairs and knees to the kitchen.

"Mrs. Bedlow?" The housekeeper was sitting in the kitchen rocker, peeling potatoes for tomorrow's hash.

"What in heaven's name?"

At the housekeeper's sharp question, Rachel's little head came up from the depths of the shawl like a turtle from a shell.

"It's Rachel, Mrs. Bedlow." Lyddie made her voice as gentle as she could. "My sister, Rachel."

She could read the warning in Mrs. Bedlow's eyes. No men, no children (except for the keeper's own) in a corporation house. But surely the woman would not have the heart . . .

"I'm begging a bath for her. She's had a long, rough journey in an ox cart, and she's chilled right through, ey Rachie?"

Rachel stiffened in her arms, but Mrs. Bedlow dropped her paring knife into the bowl of peeled potatoes, wiped her hands on her apron, and put a kettle on to boil.

It was only after they had both seen Rachel safely asleep in Lyddie's bed that Mrs. Bedlow said the words that Lyddie knew were on her mind. "It won't do, you know. She can't stay here."

"I'll get her a job. She can doff."

"You know she's not old enough or strong enough to be a doffer."

"Just till I can straighten things out," Lyddie pleaded. "Please let her stay. I'll get it all set in just a few days, ey?"

Mrs. Bedlow sighed and made to shake her head.

"I'll pay, of course. Full board. And you see how small she is. You know she won't eat a full share."

Mrs. Bedlow sat down and picked up her paring knife. Lyddie held her breath. "A week. Even then—"

"It wouldn't be more'n a fortnight. I give you my vow. I just got to write my brother."

Mrs. Bedlow looked doubtful, but she didn't say no. She just sighed and started to peel again, the long coil so thin it was almost transparent.

"I'm obliged to you, Mrs. Bedlow. I got nowhere to turn, else."

"She mustn't go outdoors. We can't have her seen about the premises."

"No, no, I swear. I'll keep her in my room. The other girls won't even know."

Mrs. Bedlow looked at Lyddie wryly. "They already know, and there's no guarantee they'll keep their peace."

"I'll beg 'em—"

"No need to coop her up more than necessary. She can come down with me during the day. I'll have Tim help her with her letters and numbers in the afternoon. She ought to be in school herself."

"She will be, Mrs. Bedlow. She will be. Soon as I can get things worked out. I swear upon my life—"

"You need to watch your language, my girl. Set an example for the little one."

"I thank you, Mrs. Bedlow. You'll not be sorry, I promise."

She wrote Charlie that night after curfew in the flickering light of a forbidden stub of candle.

Dear Brother Charles,

I hope you are well. I am sorry to trouble you with sad news, but Uncle Judah come tonight to Lowell and brung Rachel to me. They have put our mother to the asylum at Brattleboro. Now they are thinking to sell the farm. You must go and stop them. You are the man of the family. Judah won't pay me no mind. They got to listen to you. I got more than one hundred dollars to the det. Do not let them sell, Charlie. I beg you. I don't know what to do with Rachel. Children are not allowed in corporation house. If I can I will take her home, but I got to have a home to go to. It is up to you, Charlie. Please I beg you stop Uncle Judah.

Yr. loving sister,
Lydia Worthen

She could hardly keep her mind on her work. What was the use of it all anyway if the farm was gone? But it couldn't be! Not after all her sweating and saving. And what was she to do with Rachel? The child hadn't spoken a word since her arrival. She hadn't even cried. She seemed more dead than alive. And precious time must be spent finding her a place to stay and precious money put out for her keep—more if she was to go to school. Why couldn't the child work in the spinning room? There were Irish children down there who looked no older than seven or eight. They were earning their own way. Hadn't Lyddie herself been working hard since she was no more than a tadpole? And doffing wasn't as hard as farm work. Why those children hardly worked fifteen minutes out of the hour, just taking off the full spools and replacing them with empty ones. Then they just sat in the corner and played or chatted. Sometimes from the window on a clear day Lyddie had seen them running about the mill yard playing tag or marbles. It was an easy life compared to the farm, and still Rachel would be out of mischief and earning her own way.

As if she hadn't trouble enough, Brigid was crying again. Lyddie glanced over at the loom. Everything seemed in order, but the Irish girl was standing there, staring at the shuddering machine with tears running down her cheeks. Lyddie quickly checked her own looms before walking over and saying in the girl's ear, "What's the matter with you, ey?"

Brigid looked around startled. She bit her lip and shook her head.

Lyddie shrugged. It was just as well if the girl learned to bear her own troubles.

Mr. Marsden stopped Lyddie at the stairs on the way to breakfast. Her heart knotted. How could he have heard about Rachel already? Had one of the other girls tattled so soon? They were jealous of her, Lyddie knew. She was the best operator on the floor. But it was not about Rachel that Mr. Marsden wished to speak, it was about the wretched Irish girl. "You must tell her," he said, "that she must get her speed up. I can't keep her on, even as a spare hand, unless she can maintain a proper pace."

Why didn't he tell her himself? He was the overseer. Brigid did not belong to her. She hadn't asked for a spare hand—hadn't wanted one—and now he was trying to shove the responsibility off on her.

She spoke to Brigid after the break. "He says you'll have to speed up or he can't keep you on."

The girl's eyes widened in fear, reminding Lyddie, oh cuss it, of Rachel's silent face as the child sat crouched within herself in the corner of Mrs. Bedlow's kitchen. "Oh, tarnation," she hollered in Brigid's ear, "I'll help you. We'll do the five looms together for a few days—just till you get on better, ey?"

The girl smiled faintly, still frightened.

"And keep your mind on your blooming work, you hear? We can't have you catching your hair or being hit in the head by a flying shuttle because you're being stup—because your mind is someplace else."

Fresh tears started in the girl's eyes, but she bit her lip again and nodded. Lyddie could see Diana smiling approval. Good thing she couldn't hear me, Lyddie thought wryly. She wouldn't be thinking I was so kindly then.

By the seven o'clock bell, Brigid was looking a little less distraught, and Mr. Marsden came past to pat both girls proudly. Lyddie sighed and hardly bothered to dodge him. She had gotten off the fewest pieces in one day since she'd had four looms, and she still had to go home to the burden of silent little Rachel.

"Well, it won't do," said Mrs. Bedlow. "She won't talk to either Tim or me. Not a word. Just sits trembling in the corner like a frozen mouse."

"Did she manage to eat anything?"

"Did she manage to eat? She eats like she hasn't had food in a month of Sundays. I fed her with Tim. She out ate him! And he a growing boy. But never a word through it all—just shovels it in like there'll never be another plateful this side of the grave."

Lyddie looked at the housekeeper's face, pinched with anger, and then down at the top of Rachel's head. The child was trembling—like Oliver, she thought. Like Oliver.

For more? That boy will be hung. I know that boy will be hung.

Oh Rachie, Rachie. I don't want to think of you hungry. "I'll pay you more," she promised Mrs. Bedlow.

"It isn't the money . . ." But it was quite clear to Lyddie that it was indeed the money in addition to the risk, so Lyddie vowed to fetch payment from the bank the very next day. She had to buy time—at least until she heard from Charlie.

When she had finished her own supper, she fetched Rachel from the kitchen, took her out to the privy, and then led her by hand up the staircase to the bedroom. All of this was accomplished with neither of them saying a word aloud, although inside Lyddie's head lengthy conversations were bouncing about. As she tucked the quilt about the child, she tried some of her practiced lines aloud. "What did you do today, Rachie?" "Did Tim make you do some schoolwork?" "Ain't Mrs. Bedlow funny?" "She's all right, ey, just scared to break a rule . . . We got to do what the corporation says, you know, 'cause if we don't we're out of a job, and then what would we do, ey?" There was no answer. She hadn't expected any, still . . . "You musn't be worried, Rachie, Judah can't sell the farm. Charlie and me, we won't let him. We're keeping it for Papa"— was there a flicker of life in the eyes?—"and Mama—and Charlie and Rachie and Lyddie too." Did she just imagine the child had relaxed a little against the pillow, or was it a trick of the candlelight?

Maybe if she read aloud, as Betsy had to her. She opened *Oliver Twist* and commenced. When Rachel fell asleep she didn't know. Lyddie was lost in the comfort of the familiar words. When the bell rang, she blew out the candle and lay in the darkness, feeling the presence of the small body nearby. What could she do? Where could she turn for help? She couldn't keep Rachel here, and yet she, Lyddie, must live in a corporation house to keep her job. And without her job, what good could she do for any of them? But how could she put this little lost child out with strangers? She cursed her aunt and uncle—what could they have been thinking of to bring the child here? And yet, wasn't she better off here with Lyddie, who loved her, than with those two, who must not have given her enough to eat? Poor little Rachel. Poor old Lyddie. She heaved herself over in bed. She had to sleep. There was nothing she could do until she heard from Charlie. Surely Charlie could stop Judah from selling the farm, and then, debt or no debt, she'd take Rachel home. Let them try to get her off that land again. Just let them try.

In her uneasy sleep she saw the bear again, but, suddenly, in the midst of his clumsy thrashing about, he threw off the pot and was transformed, leaping like a spring buck up into the loft where they were huddled. And she could not stare him down.

16
Fever

Taking the money from the bank was like having a rooted tooth yanked from her jaw. Then, the most painful part past, she pressed two whole dollars into Mrs. Bedlow's hand before going out on the town to buy Rachel shoes and shawl and to order a dress made for her. Having spent that much, Lyddie squandered fifty pence more to get the child a beginning reader and a small paper volume of verses that the bookseller recommended. All told, Lyddie had spent more than two weeks' wages. There was less than a dollar in her pocket now left from the princely sum she had withdrawn. She tried not to think on it. It was for Rachel, wasn't it? How could she begrudge the child?

The very next day Brigid was slower than ever, and it was all that Lyddie could do to keep from screaming. Time after time she took the shuttle from the girl's clumsy hands, sucked the thread through from the bobbin, and threw it into the race, raging that a machine should stand idle for even a few seconds. Brigid was on the brink of tears all day.

At last Lyddie exploded when once again the girl's inattention caused a snarl and a ruined piece. "You must mind, girl!" she shouted. "Forget everything else but the loom."

"But I canna forget," Brigid cried out. "Me mother sick unto death and no money for a doctor."

"Here!" She snatched all the change from her apron pocket and stuffed it into Brigid's. "Here. That's for the doctor. Now— mind the machine, ey?"

The next few days went better than those before. She coaxed a few words from Rachel, and the suggestion of a smile, when she read aloud from the book of verses.

> "Doctor Foster went to Gloucester
> In a shower of rain;
> He stepped in a puddle
> Right up to his middle,
> And never went there again."

"Well," said Lyddie, "that's mud season in Vermont, ey?" And Rachel smiled. Encouraged, Lyddie tried to make a rhyme for Rachel herself.

> "Uncle Judah went to Bermuda
> In the April rain
> He sunk in the ooze
> Right up to his snooze
> And never was heard of again."

This time there was no mistaking the smile.

Work was going better as well. Brigid was pathetically grateful for her gift. She beat Lyddie to work in the mornings and had two of the machines oiled and gleaming before Lyddie even entered the room.

Mr. Marsden was very pleased. By Thursday, he smiled across the room continually. Lyddie resolved not to glance his way, but she could see without looking the little rosebud mouth fixed in its prissy bow.

How hot the room seemed. Of course it was always hot and steamy, but somehow . . . Perhaps if she hadn't been burning up she could have kept her head, but she was so hot, so exhausted that Thursday in May, she wasn't prepared, she had no defenses. He stopped her and made her wait until everyone had gone—just when she felt she must lie down or faint, he stopped her and put both his fat white hands heavily on either sleeve, dragging his weight on her arms. He was saying something as well, but her head was pounding and she couldn't make it out. What did he want with her? She had to go. She had to see Rachel. Her whole body was on fire. She needed a cool cloth for her head. And yet he kept holding on to her. She tried to stare him down, but her eyes were burning in their sockets. Let me go! She wanted to cry. She tried to pull back from him, but he clutched tighter. He was bringing his strange little mouth closer and closer to her fiery face.

She murmured something about not feeling well, but it made his eyes grow soft and his arm go all around her shoulder.

What made her do it? Illness? Desperation? She'd never know. But she raised her booted foot and stomped her heel down with all her might. He gave a cry, and, dropping his arms, doubled over. It was all the time she needed. She stumbled down the stairs and across the yard, nearly falling at last into the door of Number Five. He had not tried to follow.

She did not go to work the next day or for many days thereafter. Her fever raged, and she was out of her mind with it. Once, she realized that someone was putting a cold cloth on her forehead, and she raised her arm to bring it down over her burning eyelids. A tiny cool hand rested on her hot one and stroked it timidly. Somewhere, at a great distance, she heard a small voice croon: "There, there." And then her heavy arm was lifted and put back gently under the quilt.

Dr. Morris was summoned. She tried to protest. She couldn't waste money on doctors, but if the words came out at all, they came out too thickly for anyone to understand.

The bell rang, but it was far away now. It no longer rang for her. People came in and out of the darkened room. Sometimes Mrs. Bedlow was spooning broth into her, sometimes another of the boarders. Diana was there, and Brigid, though who would have sent for them?

Brigid had brought some Irish concoction that Mrs. Bedlow seemed to be trying to refuse, but the girl would not leave until she had been allowed to spoon some of it into the patient's mouth. And always, whenever Lyddie swam up the fiery pool out into consciousness, she knew that Rachel was there beside her.

She'll get sick, Lyddie tried to protest. Make her go away. Or move me to the infirmary. She's too frail. But either she never got the words out, or no one could or would understand, for whenever she was in her right mind, Rachel was there.

She woke one morning with a start. The bell was clanging, banging away at her dully aching head. She sat up abruptly. The room swooped and dipped about her. More slowly, she swung her legs over the side of the bed, but when she tried to stand, she fell over like a newborn calf. "Rachel," she called. "Help me. I got to go to work."

Rachel raised up from the other bed. "You're awake!" she cried. "Lyddie, you didn't die!"

She fell back onto her pillow. "No," she said weakly. "Not yet. We can stil hop."

17
Doffer

It had been two weeks since she fell ill, and Dr. Morris still refused to let her return to work. Her mind roared protest, but her legs could hardly carry her to the privy. Her body had never betrayed her before. She despised its weakness, and every day she heard the first bell and ordered herself up and dressed, but she would only be up a few minutes, not even through washing herself at the basin, before the sweat broke out on her forehead from the effort, and she was obliged to let Rachel help her back to bed.

There was too much time in bed. She slept and slept and still there were hours awake to worry when her mind skimple-skombled back on itself like threads in a snarled loom. Why hadn't Charlie written? She should have heard from him long ago. Perhaps her letter had been lost. That was it. She sat straight up.

"Better rest, Lyddie." Rachel was there as always. "The doctor said."

"Get me some paper and my pen and ink from the box there—the little one on top of the bandbox. I must write Charlie again."

Rachel obeyed, but even as she handed Lyddie the writing materials, she protested. "You ain't s'posed to worry, Lyddie. Doctor said."

Lyddie put her hand on Rachel's head. Her hair was soft as goose down. "It's all right, Rachie. I'm much better, ey? Nearly all well now."

Rachel's brow furrowed, but her eyes were clear, not the dead, blank eyes of her arrival. Lyddie stroked her hair. "I had me such a good nurse. I couldn't have believed it."

Rachel smiled and nodded at the writing box. "Tell Charlie," she said.

"I'll be sure to," Lyddie said. "He'll be monstrous proud."

By the next week she was feeling truly ready to go back to work and remembering with every breath her last act at the factory. Merciful heavens. There was probably no work to go back to. Had she really? Had she truly stomped on Mr. Marsden's foot with her boot heel? She hardly knew whether to laugh or cry. She sent a note to Brigid—most of the girls were wary of speaking to Diana under Mr. Marsden's nose—asking her and Diana to stop over after supper.

That evening both Diana and Brigid came as she hoped. Brigid brought more soup from her now fully recovered mother and a half bottle of Dr. Rush's Infallible Health Pills. "Me mother swears by them," she said, blushing.

Diana handed Lyddie a paperbound book—*American Notes for General Circulation*—by Mr. Charles Dickens. "Since you're such an admirer of the gentleman, I thought you might like to see what he wrote about factory life in Lowell," she said. "I suppose he was comparing us to the satanic mills of England—anyhow, it's a bit romantical, as they say."

A book. By Mr. Dickens. "How did you know—"

"My dear, anyone who copies a book out page by page and pastes it to her frame . . ."

Lyddie sent Rachel and Brigid down to beg a cup of tea from Mrs. Bedlow. "Diana, I got to ask you. Has Mr. Marsden said anything of me?"

"Well, of course. He missed you at once. You're his best girl."

Lyddie felt her face go crimson.

"I told him I'd ask after you. That's when I learned how ill you were. A lot of the girls have been out with this fever—especially the Irish. There've been many deaths in the Acre."

Lyddie looked away, out the tiny dirty window of the bedroom. Thank you, God. How could I leave my baby girl?

Diana reached over from where she was sitting on the edge of the other bed and put her hand lightly on Lyddie's arm. "I'm grateful you were spared, Lyddie," she said softly.

Lyddie pressed her lips together and gave a little nod. "I reckon I'm too ornery to die."

"I wouldn't be surprised."

"Can you recollect—can you remember just what Mr. Marsden said when he asked about me?"

"He didn't speak directly to me. He doesn't like to think that you and I are friends, you know, but I know he was worried. He wouldn't want to lose you."

"So I still got a place?"

Diana looked at her as though she were crazy. "Why on earth not?"

"I stomped his foot."

"You what?"

"I was all a fever, only I didn't know, ey, and he tried to hold me after the rest had gone. He wouldn't let me go, so I—I stomped down on his foot."

Diana threw her head back and laughed out loud.

"It ain't a joke. He'll have my place for it."

"No, no," she said, trying to recover. "No," she said, taking out her handkerchief and wiping her eyes. "No, I don't think so. He's probably more frightened than you are. Have you ever seen Mrs. Overseer Marsden, Lyddie? If word ever got to that august lady . . ." She stopped laughing and lowered her voice, her ear cocked toward the open door. "Nonetheless, I wouldn't make attacking the overseer a regular practice, my dear. Do be more discreet in the future—that is, if you want to stay on at the corporation. The day may come when Mr. Marsden would welcome any excuse to let you go." She smiled wryly. "It sounds as though I'm advising you not to sign any petitions or consort with any known radicals."

"But maybe he meant nothing. I was burnt up with the fever. Maybe I mistook kindness for—for—" She grimaced. "You know I'm not the kind of girl men look at that way. I'm plain as plowed sod."

Diana raised an eyebrow, but Rachel and Brigid were at the door with the tea, so she said nothing more.

I'll pretend, thought Lyddie, as she tried to unsnarl her brain over the steaming cup, I'll pretend I was crazy from the fever and didn't know what I was doing—can't even remember what I did.

"I want to be a doffer, Lyddie," Rachel said. Lyddie had brushed her sister's curls and was weaving them into plaits. Rachel wanted to pin her hair up like the big girls in the house, but Lyddie insisted that the braids hang down. She couldn't bear for Rachel to look like a funny little make-believe woman. "Brigid says her little sister is a doffer and she's no bigger than me."

"Oh Rachel. You need to go to school." She loved to braid Rachel's hair, but was suddenly ashamed that she had only string to bind it with. She should have splurged on a bit of ribbon. Rachel was so pretty, for all her being too thin. She ought to have bright bows to set off the two silky curls at the end of each plait. They would brighten her drab little dress. But ribbons cost money, and string bound the hair just as well. She twisted each curl around her index finger and gave it a final brush. "We got to get you into school. You don't want to grow ignorant as your Lyddie."

"You ain't ignorant a-tall. I seed you read."

"You want I should read to you, Rachie?"

"No. I want you should let me be a doffer."

"We'll have to wait and see, ey? When we hear from Charlie . . ."

But they didn't hear from Charlie. They heard from Quaker Stevens.

Dear Sister Worthen,
    Thy brother asked me to look into the sale of thy farm. All inquiry has come to naught, but as I have business in thy uncle's neighborhood on Wednesday next, I will inquire directly at that time. I trust thee and the little one are in good health. Son Luke asks to be remembered to thee.
                                    Thy friend and neighbor,
                                    Jeremiah Stevens

She tried not to feel angry at Charlie for not writing to her himself. He had, after all, done the sensible thing. To the law and their uncle, they were only children. Judah would have to listen to Quaker Stevens. He was a man of substance. She was glad to know that Luke had gotten safely home. She had finally realized that the freight he had come to fetch was human.

The letter meant, though, that she could wait no longer. Something would have to be done about Rachel. The promised fortnight had passed, and she must go back to work herself on the morrow. She sent Rachel to the bedroom, stuffed the letter in her apron pocket, and went into the kitchen.

She didn't start with the request, but with an offer of help to fix dinner. Mrs. Bedlow was always grateful for an extra hand in the kitchen, even though the house was now down to only twenty girls.

"You give me more than the fortnight, Mrs. Bedlow, and I

am obliged," she said, once the cabbage had been chopped and the bread sliced.

"You were near to death, Lyddie. I'm not without heart."

"Indeed not." Lyddie smiled as warmly as she knew how. "You been more'n good to me and mine. Which is why I dare—"

"It won't do, you know. I can't keep her on indefinitely."

"But if she was a doffer—"

"She's hardly more than a baby."

"She's small, but she's a worker. Didn't she nurse me, ey?"

"She pulled you through. I wouldn't have warranted it—"

"Could you ask the agent for me? Just until I got things set with my brother? All I want to do is take her home. It wouldn't be for long, I swear. Meantime, I've not the heart to set her out with strangers."

Mrs. Bedlow was weakening. Lyddie could read it in the sag of her face. She pressed on, eagerly. "It won't be more than a few weeks, and I'd pay extra, I would. I know it's hard for you with only twenty girls here regular—"

"I'll speak to the agent, but I can't promise you—"

"I know, I know. But if you'll just ask for me. She's a fine little worker, and so eager to make good."

"I can't promise anything—"

"Would you go now and ask?"

"Now? I'm in the middle of fixing dinner—"

"I'll finish for you. Please. So I can take her over when I go back to work tomorrow . . ."

It was arranged. Lyddie suspected that Mrs. Bedlow had added a few years and several pounds in her description of Rachel to the agent, but a skeptical look was all she got from the overseer on the spinning floor when she presented Rachel for work the next morning. And Rachel looked so bright and eager and smiled so sweetly that even the skeptical look melted, and she was sent, skipping down the aisle, to meet the other doffers under the care of a kindly middle-aged spinner.

Slowly, Lyddie climbed the flight of stairs to the weaving room. Her worry for Rachel had pushed aside, for a time, her own fears of seeing Mr. Marsden again. She didn't dare look in his direction, but went straight to her looms where Brigid was already at work, cleaning and oiling.

"You're looking much the rosier," Brigid said. How pretty the girl was with her light brown hair and eyes clear blue as a bright February sky after snow. It was the smile, though, that transformed her into a real beauty. Lyddie smiled back. She did not envy other women their good looks. And even if she had been so inclined, she would never begrudge this bounty of nature to one so poor in everything else.

"We covered the machines as best we could while you were gone, me and Diana. Though"—she smiled apologetically— "you'll see from your wage, the work was not near what it would be, had you been here."

It was all they had time to say before Mr. Marsden stepped on his stool and pulled the cord that set the room to roaring and shaking. Lyddie jumped, then laughed. How quickly she'd forgotten the noise! Within minutes she had settled in and forgotten everything else—Mr. Marsden, her weakness, the farm, Charlie, even Rachel. It was good to be back with her beasts again. She belonged among them somehow.

By the breakfast bell she was almost too tired to eat. She would, if she could have chosen, sat out the break in the window alcove, but that would leave her alone on the floor. She glanced at Mr. Marsden and hurried toward the stairs. He didn't speak to her. It was as if nothing had occurred between them, except that he never came over to her loom to pat and encourage her. Not once.

She managed to eat breakfast, or some of it. Rachel was

stuffing herself like a regular factory girl, talking excitedly at the same time. She stopped only to look at Lyddie and say through her full mouth, "Eat, Lyddie. You got to eat and grow strong."

So it was she got through breakfast and dinner, but by supper she could only manage a few bites of stew before she dragged herself up to bed. Fatigue was like a toothache in her bones. She would have cursed her weakness, had she the strength.

Each day, though, she was a little stronger. At first she could not feel it, no more than a body can feel itself grow taller. But by the end of the week, she found that she had eaten a full plate at supper and was lingering in the parlor with Rachel, who was watching, fascinated, as a phrenologist sought to sell his services to the girls.

"Please, Lyddie," Rachel begged. "Let's have our heads done."

"I know about my head, Rachel. Why should I pay good money to find out it's plain as sod and stubborn as a mule?"

"And such a skinflint a penny would freeze to your fist before you'd spend it," the phrenologist snapped. "I give you that reading for free. Not that there's hope you'd pay."

The other girls in the parlor tittered. Even Lyddie tried to smile, but Rachel was indignant. "She's not mean. She's going to buy me ribbons," she declared. "Come on, Lyddie," she added, taking her hand. "Let's go read the book you bought me."

The girls laughed again, but more gently. They had never cared much for Lyddie, whom they knew to be close with her money and her friendships, but Rachel was rapidly becoming their pet.

How dry her life had been before Rachel came. It was like springs of water in the desert to have her here. She kissed her head that night before she tucked her in. "You don't think your Lyddie is a cheap old spinster, ey?"

Rachel was furious all over again. "You're the best sister in the world!"

Lyddie blew out the candle. She lay listening to Rachel's even breathing and heard in her memory the sounds of birds in the spring woods. If only she could hear from Charlie, Lyddie's happiness would be complete. The money was growing again. She had nearly caught up with the wages lost by her illness, and even though Rachel made only a pittance, it paid her room and board. She had seldom been happier.

She woke in the night, puzzled. She thought she had heard Betsy again—that wretched hacking sound that sawed through her rib cage straight into her heart. And then she was wide awake and knew it to be Rachel.

It was only a cold. Surely it was nothing. She would be over it in a week. See, the child seemed bright-eyed and lively as ever. If she were sick, really sick . . . Lyddie kept the knowledge of the night cough tight inside herself, but the fear grew like a tumor. She began to lie awake listening for the awful sound, until finally, she knew she must send the child away—anywhere, just so she was not breathing this poison air.

It will break my heart to send the child away. Lyddie could not bear the thought. It might break Rachel's heart as well. She has been sent away too often in her short life. Look, she dotes on me. Me, tough and mean as I be. She clings to me more than she ever did our mother. She needs me.

Lyddie did not know what to do, and she was too terrified to ask. No one must know. She fed Rachel the pills Brigid had brought her. She had no faith in them, but she must try. She fixed plasters for the child's chest, trying to turn it into a game, desperate to hide her own terror. And she was succeeding, wasn't she? Rachel seemed happy as ever and carefree as a kitten. Caught in a spasm of coughing, she made light of it. "Silly cough," she said. "All the girls have them."

Lyddie mustn't worry. Summer was here. The weather was warm. Rachel would be over it soon. They'd take July off. Go back to the farm, the two of them. But it was a vain dream, Lyddie knew. There would be nothing to eat there. The cow was gone and no crops planted.

Triphena. She would send Rachel to Triphena. But Triphena meant Mistress Cutler as well as that lonely, airless attic. How could she do to Rachel at eight what her mother had done to her at thirteen? It had been hard even then. And so very lonely. She hadn't realized how lonely until now—now that she was no longer alone.

Then one evening in late June—she had just read Rachel to sleep—Tim knocked on the door. "A visitor for you, Lyddie," he said. "In the parlor."

18
Charlie at Last

She hardly knew him. He was not so much taller, but bigger somehow, foreign. He wore homespun, but it was well tailored to his body. His brown hair was combed neatly against his head, and a carpetbag hung from his right hand.

"Sister," he said quietly, and the voice was one she had never heard before and would not have known for his.

"Sister," he repeated, his voice cracking on the words, "it's me, Charles."

"Yes," she said. "Charles. So—you come."

He smiled then. She looked in vain for the funny, serious little boy she knew. He wasn't thirteen yet. How could he have discarded that little child so quickly?

He glanced around the crowded room. All the staring faces quickly dived back into their sewing or knitting or conversation. "I took the railroad car," he said in quiet pride. "The stage into New Hampshire, to Concord, and then all the rest of the way by train." Then he grinned like a child, but not the child she remembered. Not quite.

She didn't know what to say. She cared nothing for railroads, those dangerous, dirty things. It was the farm she ached to know about. "Well," she said at last, "you must be tired, ey?"

She cast about the parlor for two free chairs. At her glance, three girls rose and abandoned theirs in the far corner of the room beyond the dining tables. She thanked them and led him over. It was she who felt the need to sit.

"Well," she said, arranging her apron on her lap. "Well, then?" It was as much of a question as she could manage.

"I got good news, Lyddie," he said, a little of the boy she knew creeping into his voice. Her heart rose.

"The Phinneys have taken me on as full apprentice."

"Ey?"

"More than that, truly. They treat me like their own. They don't have no child but me."

"You got a family," she said faintly.

"You'll always be my sister, Lyddie. I don't forget that. It's just . . ." He put the carpetbag on the floor and laid his cap carefully on top. His hands were big now, too large for his body. Finally he looked up at her. "It's just—I don't have to worry every morning when I get up and every night when I lie abed. I just do my work, and every day, three times, the food is there. When the work is slack, I go to school. It's a good life they give me, Lyddie—"

She wanted to scream out at him, remind him how hard she had worked for him, how hard she had tried, but she only said softly, "I wanted to do for you, Charlie. I tried—"

"Oh Lyddie, I know," he said, leaning toward her. "I know. But it waren't fair to you. You only a girl, trying to be father and mother and sister to us all. It were too much. This'll be best for you, too, ey. Don't you see?"

No! she wanted to howl. No! What will be the use of me, then? But she kept her lips pressed together against such a cry. At last she said, "There's Rachel . . ."

He smiled again, his grown-up smile that turned him into a stranger. "I have good news there, too. Mrs. Phinney asked me to bring Rachel back. She craves a daughter as well. And she'll be so good to her, you'll see. She even sent a dress. She made it herself for Rachel to wear on the train. With a bonnet even." His eyes went to the carpetbag beside the chair. "She's never had a proper Ma, Rachel."

She has me. Oh Charlie, I ain't perfect, but I do my best. Can't you see? I done my best for you. She's all I got left now. How can I let her go? But even as she stormed within herself, she knew she had no choice. Like the rusty blade through her heart she felt it. If she stays here with me, she will die. If I cling to her, I will be her death.

She heard her own voice, calm as morning after a storm, no, quiet as death, say, "When will you be leaving?"

"The train leaves Lowell at five minutes after seven of the morning. I'll come to fetch her at half past six."

"I'll have her ready before I go to work." She stood. There was nothing more to be said.

He stood, too, cap in hand, wanting, she knew, to say more, but not knowing quite how. She waited.

"About the farm . . ." he began.

The farm. A few minutes before she had thought it was all she cared about. Now it had ceased to matter.

"Uncle Judah's bound and determined to sell."

Lyddie nodded. "Well," she said, "so be it."

He grinned wryly. "For a man who says the Lord is set to end the whole Creation at any minute, he's got a powerful concern for the vain things of this world." She realized he was trying to be funny, so she attempted a smile.

"But I near forgot . . ." He reached into an inside pocket and took out a sealed letter.

Lyddie stared at it. "He ain't sending me money?"

"Who?"

"Uncle."

"Oh, no, not him. He says anything from the sale is rightly

his for taking care of Ma and the babies all this time. No. This here is a letter." He handed it to her, studying her face the while. "From Luke."

"Luke who?"

"Lyddie! Our friend, Luke. Our neighbor Luke Stevens." He seemed shocked. He couldn't know she was two lifetimes away from the day Luke had driven them to the village and at least one lifetime from the day the Quaker boy had stood on the doorstep of Number Five in his peculiar disguise.

She tucked the letter in her apron pocket. "Thank you," she said, "and good-bye, I reckon. I'll not be here in the morning when you come."

"It'll be all right, Lyddie. It'll be best for us all, ey?" His voice was anxious. "It'll work out best for you, as well."

"You forgot your bag," she said.

"No, that's for Rachel." He picked it up and handed it to her. He put out his hand as if to shake hers, but hers were tightly wrapped around the handle of the bag. She nodded instead. The next she saw him he would be taller than she, Lyddie thought. If there was a next time. She led him to the door. "Good-bye," she mouthed the words. She couldn't have spoken them aloud if she'd dared.

She climbed the stairs like an old, decrepit woman, clinging to the banister and pulling herself up step by step. Rachel was fast asleep. She would not wake her. In the candlelight she studied the lovely little face. Too thin, too pale, the skin nearly transparent. Lyddie brushed back a curl that had escaped its plait and smoothed it against Rachel's cheek. Any minute she would start to cough, her little body wracked, the bed shaking. Mrs. Phinney would keep her safe. She could go to school. She would have a good life, a real mother. And she will forget me, plain, rough, miserly Lyddie who only bought her ribbons because she was shamed to it. Will she ever know how much

I loved her? How I would have gladly laid down my life and died for her? How, O Lord, I am dying this very minute for her?

She took out the dress. It was a lovely sprigged muslin. It looked too big for Rachel's tiny frame, but the child would grow into it. She would lengthen and fatten and turn once again into a stranger. Lyddie's tears were soaking the dress. She wiped her face on her own apron skirt, then laid out the new garments—the frilly little bonnet with ribbons and lace, a petticoat fit for a wedding. A length of pink ribbon was woven in and out all around the top of the hem, wasted, pure waste where no one would ever see it. Except Rachie.

She packed the bag. It took less than a minute. Rachel had so little. She remembered the primer, and then decided to keep it. Rachel would have a new one, a better one now. She took the book of verses off the nightstand and shut it in the bag, then took it out again. She got her box of writing materials, dipped her pen in the ink, and wrote in painful, careful script on the fly leaf: "For Rachel Worthen from her sister Lydia Worthen, June 24, 1846," wiping her face carefully on her apron as she wrote so as not to blot the page.

She lay awake most of the night listening to Rachel cough, the sound rasping and sawing through her own body. But the pain of it was her salvation. She knew, if she had ever doubted before, she was absolutely certain, that Rachel must leave Lowell.

When the first bell rang, instead of waking Rachel as usual, she waited until she herself was dressed and ready to go. Then she shook her gently.

Rachel awoke at once, alarmed. "I'm late! Why did you let me sleep?"

"You got a treat today, Rachie. Charlie's come to fetch you."

"Charlie? My brother Charlie?" She was as excited as if she could really remember him. Lyddie brushed away a cobweb of envy. "He's come to take you for a visit."

"He wants me to visit him?" She was plainly thrilled, but then she caught something in Lyddie's face. "You coming too, ain't you Lyddie?"

"No, not me. I got to work, ey?" The child's face darkened. "I'll come later." She stretched out her hand. "Here, up you go, you got to get ready."

Rachel took Lyddie's hand and pulled herself upright, then threw back the covers. The child always slept under a quilt, even in the terrible summer heat. "How long will I be gone, Lyddie?"

"I don't rightly know. We both, me and Charlie, we both think you should stay awhile. Make sure you get rid of that silly cough, ey? The factory is too hot in summer, anyways. Lots of the girls take off, come July."

"Will you take off, Lyddie?" She was standing in her little night shift, scratching one leg with the bare toes of the other.

"I just might. Who knows, ey?" Lyddie wrung out the cloth over the basin and handed it to Rachel to wash.

"Come with me now, Lyddie."

"Over on the other bed is a new dress for you to put on. You got to dress fancy for riding on a train."

"A railroad train?"

"Luckiest girl I know. New dress and bonnet, train ride, holiday with a handsome man . . ." She took the cloth from Rachel's hand, tipped up the child's chin, and began to wash her upturned face. "Now you learn your letters better so you can write me all about that train ride." The bell began to ring. She turned swiftly, wringing the cloth out over the basin, her face to the wall, lest she betray herself. "He'll be here to fetch you in a hour or so," she said brightly. "So get yourself dressed and go down and ask Mrs. Bedlow to give you a extra big breakfast." She turned only long enough to give Rachel a light kiss on the cheek and then hurried out the door.

"Come soon, Lyddie." Rachel's voice followed her down the stairs. "I'll miss you."

"Be a good girl for Charlie," she called back, and rushed on down the stairs with a great clatter to erase any more sounds, any more doubts.

Rachel had been gone nearly a week when she found the letter with her name written on it in small, neat handwriting. She had stuffed it into her trunk some days before and couldn't remember at first where it had come from. She unsealed it curiously.

Dear Lyddie Worthen,
    Doubtless thy Charlie has told thee about thy farm. Although our father pled on thy behalf, thy uncle could not be moved. Thus our father put down the purchase price himself, as he has four sons and not enough land for us all.
    I have spoken with thy Charlie. He has urged me to put aside my fears and speak my heart plain. Which is that I long to earn from our father the deed to thy farm. Yet thy land would be barren without thee.
    May I dare ask thee to return? Not as sister, but as wife?
    Forgive these bold words, but I know not how to fashion pretty phrases fit for such as thee.
                                        In all respect, thy friend,
                                        Luke Stevens

What had Charlie said to the man to make him dare write such a letter? Do they think they can buy me? Do they think I will sell myself for that land? That land I have no one to take to anymore? I have nothing left but me, Lyddie Worthen—do they think I will sell her? I will not be a slave. Nor will I be his freight—some homeless fugitive that Luke Stevens must bend down his lofty Quaker soul to rescue.

She tore the letter into tiny bits and stuffed every shred of it into Mrs. Bedlow's iron cook stove, and then, to her own amazement, burst into tears.

19

Diana

She had been alone before Rachel came, but she had not known what loneliness was—this sharp pain in her breastbone dragging down into a dull, persistent heaviness. My heart is heavy, she thought. It's not just a saying. It is what is—heavy, a great stone lodged in my breast, pressing down my whole being. How can I even stand straight and look out upon the world? I am doubled over into myself and, for all the weight, find only emptiness.

Workdays dragged by with nothing to look forward to at the evening bell. Rumor had it that the corporation had slowed the clocks to squeeze even more minutes out of the long summer shift. From time to time, she wondered why she was working so hard, now that the farm was sold and Rachel and Charlie lost to her. She brushed the question aside. She worked hard because work was all she knew, all she had. Everything else that had made her know herself as Lyddie Worthen was gone. Nothing but hard work—so hard that her mind became as calloused as her hands—work alone remained. She fell into bed exhausted and only felt the full burden of her grief in dreams, which, determined as she was, she could not control.

The weavers at the Massachusetts Corporation had all refused the agent's demand that they each tend four looms and take a piece rate reduction as well. They signed a pledge in defiance and none of them backed down. The word went like a whispered wave through the Concord weaving room: "Not a girl has backed down. Not one."

Diana should have been elated. Wasn't it a victory for the Association? But when Lyddie was finally able to rouse herself from her own pain, she saw that Diana's face was drawn, the expression grim and set. Since Rachel had gone, whenever Brigid or Diana had tried to reach out to her, she had shaken them off. No one could understand her loss, she was sure. She did not have the strength to bear their vain attempts to comfort.

Then, suddenly, it was mid-July, and Lyddie realized that Diana was still at work, looking more sickly by the day. It was more than the heat of the weaving room. She's worried, Lyddie thought, she's sore troubled, and I, so bent on my own trial, never took it to mind.

Lyddie tried to speak to Diana on the stairs, but she seemed hardly to hear the greeting. Are they threatening her with dismissal? With blacklisting? A chill went through Lyddie. She thought she had nothing else to lose, but suppose Diana was to go? Diana—the one person who, from her first day on, had treated her like a proper person—the only one who had never laughed at Lyddie's queer mountain speech or demanded that she change her manners or her mind. All the girls took their burdens to Diana. She was always the one who came to help *you*. Nobody ever thought of Diana needing help.

She's ill—like Betsy and Rachel and Prudence and a host of others, Lyddie thought. She's worked here too long and too hard. How much longer could Diana last? How much longer could any of them last?

I must do something for her, Lyddie decided, give her a present. There was only one present good enough.

"Diana?" Lyddie worked her way through the jostling crowd of operatives crossing the yard. "I been thinking." She glanced around to see if anyone was listening, but all the girls were too intent on rushing home for their suppers. "About the— the—" Even now that she had made up her mind, she couldn't quite bring herself to speak the forbidden word in the very courtyard of the corporation. She took a deep breath. "I been thinking on signing."

The older girl turned to her and put her hand on Lyddie's sleeve. "Well," she said, and Lyddie couldn't quite make out the rest in the clamor of the yard, but it sounded something like: "Well, we'll see," as Diana let herself be carried away in the rushing stream of operatives.

But I mean it, thought Lyddie. I mean it.

Earlier in the spring she had known that there were girls in her own house secretly circulating the petition, but now that she had made up her mind to it, she wanted to do it for Diana. How could it be a true present otherwise? After supper she put on her bonnet and went to Diana's boardinghouse. She asked one of the girls in the front room of Number Three for Diana. "Diana Goss?" the girl asked with a sneer. "It's Tuesday. She'll be at her meeting."

"Oh."

The girl looked her up and down as though memorizing her features. Maybe the girl was a corporation spy. Stare her down, Lyddie told herself. The other was shorter than she, so when Lyddie stood tall and looked down into her eyes, the girl shifted her gaze. "It's at their reading room on Central Street." She glanced back at Lyddie. The sneer had returned. "Number Seventy-six. All are welcome. So I'm told."

In for a penny, in for a pound, thought Lyddie, and made her way into town.

The meeting had already begun. Someone was reading minutes. The forty or so girls crowded into the small room looked almost like a sewing circle, so many of the girls were doing mending or needlework.

"Hello." The young woman who seemed to be in charge interrupted the secretary's droning. "Come on in."

Lyddie stepped into the room, looking about uncertainly for a chair. To her relief she saw Diana, getting up and coming toward her. "You came," she said, her tired features relaxing into a smile. It reminded her of that first night when she had gone to see Diana, except then Diana had looked lovely and full of life. She took Lyddie to a place where there were two vacant chairs and sat beside her while the meeting carried on.

It was hard for Lyddie to follow the discussion. They were planning something for some sort of rally at the end of the month. She kept waiting for someone to mention the petition, so she could declare herself ready to sign, but no one did. At the first curfew bell, the woman in charge pronounced the meeting adjourned until the following Tuesday, and the girls broke into a buzz, gathering their sewing things together and putting on bonnets to leave.

The woman who had been in charge came over to where Lyddie was standing with Diana. She stretched out her hand. "I'm Mary Emerson," she said. "Welcome. I think this is your first time with us."

Lyddie shook the woman's hand and nodded.

"This is my friend, Lydia Worthen," Diana said. "She's thinking about joining us."

Miss Emerson turned expectantly to Lyddie. "I come to sign the—the petition," Lyddie said.

The woman cocked her head, seemingly puzzled. What was the matter with her? "The one to ask for ten-hour workdays." Why was she explaining the petition to a leader of the movement? It was crazy.

"Maybe next year," Diana was saying quietly.

"No. I made up my mind to it. I want to do it now. To-night."

"But we've already submitted it," Miss Emerson said. "We had to. Before the legislature recessed for the year."

She had at long last made up her mind to do it, and now it was too late? "But—"

"Next year," Diana repeated, "you can put your name in the very first column, if you like."

"Yes," said Miss Emerson brightly. "That's our motto— 'We'll try again.' Since four thousand names didn't convince them, next year we'll have to get eight." She gave Lyddie the kind of encouraging smile a teacher gives to a slow pupil. "We'll need all the help we can get."

Lyddie stood there, openmouthed, looking from Diana's thin face to the other woman's robust one. Too late. She'd come too late. She was always too late. Too late to save the farm. Too late to keep her family together. Too late to do for Diana the only thing she knew to do.

"We'd better get you back to Number Five," Diana was saying. Like she was some helpless child who needed tending. "You wouldn't want to be late."

They hurried down the dimly lit streets toward the Concord boardinghouses without speaking. Lyddie wanted to explain— to say she was sorry, to somehow make it up to Diana—but she didn't know how to do it.

As they neared Number Five, Diana broke the silence. "Thank you for coming tonight."

"Oh Diana, I come too late."

"You came as soon as you could."

"I'm always too late to do any good."

"Lyddie . . ." Diana was hesitating. "I'll miss you."

What was she saying? "I ain't going nowhere. I'll be right here. Next year and the next."

"No. *I'm* the one who'll be leaving."

"But where would you be going?" Diana had always said that the mill was her family.

"Boston, I think."

"I don't understand. Are you ailing?"

"Lyddie, if I don't leave soon—right away, in fact—I'll be dismissed."

"It's because of the cussed petition. They're trying to get you—"

"No. Not that. I wish it were." They had stopped walking and stood several yards away from the steps of Number Five. They both watched the heavy door swing open and glimpsed the light inside as two girls hurried in to beat the final bell. "It's because . . . Oh Lyddie, don't despise me . . ."

"I could never do that!" How could Diana say such a thing?

"Lyddie, I've been, oh, I don't know—foolish? wicked?"

"What are you talking about? You could never be—"

"Oh, yes." She was silent for a moment as though sifting the words she needed from the chaff of her thoughts. "I'm going to have a child, Lyddie."

"A what?" Her voice had dropped to a stunned whisper. She tried to search Diana's features, but it was too dark to read her expression. "Who done this to you?" she asked finally.

"Oh Lyddie, no one 'done' it to me."

"Then he'll marry you, ey?"

"He—he's not free to marry. There's a wife . . . in Concord. She wouldn't come to live here in a factory town. Though her father is one of the owners." Diana's laugh was short and harsh.

It was that doctor. Lyddie was sure of it. He looked so kind and gentle and all the time . . . "But what will you do?" She could hear now the shrillness in her voice. She tried to tone it down. "Where can you go?"

"I've got some savings, and he's—he's determined to help as he can. I'll find work. I'll—we'll manage—the baby and I."

"It ain't right."

"I'll need to go soon. I can't bring dishonor on the Associ-

153

ation. Any whisper of this, and our enemies will dance like dervishes with delight." She could hear the grim amusement in Diana's voice. "I won't hand them a weapon to destroy us. Not if I can possibly help it."

"How can I help you? Oh Diana, I been so blind—"

She touched Lyddie's cheek lightly. "Let's just pray everyone has been as blind. I'll write you, if I may. Tell you how things go—"

"You been so good to me—"

"I'll miss you, little Lyddie." The final bell began to clang. "Quick. Slip in before they lock you out."

"Diana—" But the older girl pushed her toward the door and hurried away down the street toward Number Three.

The word passed around the floor next morning was that Diana Goss had left, snatching an honorable dismissal while she could still get it. Much more of her radical doings and she would have been blacklisted, or so the rumors went.

20
B Is for Brigid

Brigid had two looms now and would soon be ready for a third. She stood between them proudly, the sweat pouring from her forehead in concentration. If she would wear less clothing—but no, the girls from the Acre wore the same layers of dress, summer and winter. Still, despite her craziness, Brigid was turning into a proper operative.

Mr. Marsden hardly came past Lyddie's looms these days. When their eyes met by chance, it was as though they had never been introduced. Earlier, his coldness had worried her. She feared then that he might find some reason to dismiss her, so she had been scrupulous to observe every regulation to the letter. As the days went on, she became less anxious about Mr. Marsden's state of mind, much preferring his coolness to the rosebud smiles and little pats she had endured before her illness.

She treated herself to some more books. In honor of Ezekial Freeman—what a handsome name her friend had chosen for himself—she bought *Narrative of the Life of Frederick Douglass: An American Slave Written by Himself* and a Bible. Both volumes became a quiet comfort to her Sunday loneliness, because as she read them she could hear Ezekial's rich, warm voice filling the darkness of the cabin.

She had liked Mr. Dickens's account of his travels in America—all but the Lowell part. It was, as Diana had warned her, romantical. There was no mention in its rosy descriptions of sick lungs or blacklisting or men with wives at Concord.

July wore on its weary way into August. It seemed a century since the summer just a year ago when she had read and reread *Oliver Twist* and dreamed of home. She had been such a child then—such a foolish, unknowing child. As always, many of the New England operatives had gone home. Brigid took on her third loom. More Irish girls came on as spare hands, some of the machines simply stood idle. The room was quieter. Lyddie took to copying out passages from Mr. Douglass and the Bible to paste on her looms.

She liked the Psalms best. "I will lift up mine eyes unto the hills . . ." and "By the rivers of Babylon there we sat down, yea, we wept, when we remembered Zion . . ." The Psalms were poetry, no, songs that rode the powerful rhythm of the looms.

Sometimes she composed her own. "By the rivers of Merrimack and Concord there we sat down, yea, we wept, when we remembered . . ." I must forget, she thought. I must forget them all. I cannot bear the remembering.

Lyddie was strong again. Her body no longer betrayed her into exhaustion by the end of the day, and she was past shedding tears for what might have been. It was a relief, she told herself, not to carry the burden of debt or, what was worse, the welfare of other persons. A great yoke had been lifted from her shoulders, had it not? And someday the stone would be taken from her breast as well.

Between them, she and Brigid coached several of the new spare hands, all of them wearing far too much clothing in the suffocating heat. "But me mither says me capes will cape me cool," one of the girls insisted. Lyddie let it be. She hadn't managed to persuade Brigid to take off her silly capes, how could she expect to persuade the new girls? Still, she was more patient with them than she had ever been with poor Brigid at the beginning. She had to be. Brigid herself was a paragon of gentleness, teaching the new girls all that Lyddie and Diana had taught her, never raising her voice in irritation or complaint.

Lyddie watched her snip off a length of thread from a bobbin and lead one of the clumsier girls over to the window and show her in the best light how to tie a weaver's knot. It was exactly what Lyddie remembered doing, but she knew, to her shame, that her own face had betrayed exasperation, while Brigid's was as gentle as that of a ewe nuzzling her lamb.

She smiled ruefully at Brigid as the girl returned to her own looms. Brigid smiled back broadly. "She's a bit slow, that one."

"We're all allowed to be fools the first week or two," she said, hearing Diana's voice in her head. There had been a short note from Diana telling her not to worry—that she had found a place in a seamstress's shop. But how could she not be anxious for her?

"Aye," Brigid was continuing sadly, "but I'm a fool yet." She nodded at the Psalm pasted on Lyddie's loom. "And you such a scholar."

Lyddie slid her fingers under the paper to loosen the paste and handed it to Brigid. "Here," she said, "for practice. I'll make another for myself."

Brigid shook her head. "It will do me no good. I might as well be blind, you know."

"But I sent you a note once—"

"I took it straight away to Diana to read to me."

"You've learned your letters at least?"

Shamefaced, the girl shook her head.

Lyddie sighed. She couldn't take Brigid on to teach, but how could she begrudge her a chance to start? She made papers for the girl to post.

"*A* is for agent." Beside it was a crude picture of a man in a beaver hat—the stern high priest of those invisible Boston gods who had created the corporations and to whom all in Lowell daily sacrificed their lives.

"*B* is for bobbin and Brigid, too." *B* was instantly mastered.

"*C* is for carding."

"*D* is for drawing in." She went on, using as far as possible words Brigid knew from factory life. Each day Lyddie gave her three new papers to post and learn, and, at the end of the day, to take home and practice.

So it was that day by day, without intending to be, Lyddie found herself bound letter by letter, word by word, sentence by sentence, page by page, until it was, "Come by when you've had your supper, and we'll work on the reader together." Or on a Sunday afternoon: "Meet me by the river, and I'll bring paper and pens for practice."

She did not go to Brigid's house. She was not afraid to go into the Acre. She was not frightened by rumors of robberies and assaults, but, somehow, she was reluctant to go for Brigid's sake. She did not want Brigid to have to be ashamed of the only home she had.

At last a letter came from Charlie. She had not allowed herself to look for one, but when it came she realized how she had longed to hear—just to be reminded that she had not been altogether forgotten.

Dear Sister Lyddie,

(Charlie did make his letters well!)

We are fine. We hope you are well, too. Rachel began school last month. Her cough is nearly gone, and she is growing quite fat with Mrs. Phinney's cooking.

Luke Stevens says he has had no reply. Do think kindly

on him, Lyddie. You need someone to watch out for you as well.

> Your loving brother,
> Charles Worthen

She almost tore this letter up, but stopped at the first tear. She had nearly ripped the page across Charlie's name.

September came. Some of the New England girls had returned to the weaving room, though the room now was mostly Irish. No Diana, of course, though there was something in Lyddie that kept waiting for her, that kept expecting to see the tall, quiet form moving toward her through the lint-filled room. She had taken something from the weaving floor with her going. There was no quiet center left in the tumult.

A letter arrived in September, on thick, expensive paper, the address decked out in curlicues. "We regret to inform you of the death of Maggie M. Worthen . . ." They hadn't even got her name right. Poor Mama. Nothing ever right for her in life or death. Lyddie squeezed her eyes closed and tried to picture her mother's face. She could see the thin, restless form rocking back and forth before the fire, the hair already streaked with gray. But the face was blurred. She had been gone so long from them. Gone long before she died.

Fall came. Not the raucous patchwork of the Green Mountains, but the sedate brocade of a Massachusetts city. The days began to shorten. Lyddie went to work in darkness and came back to supper in darkness. The whale oil lamps stayed on nearly the whole day in the factory, so water buckets were kept filled on every floor. Fire was a constant dread while the lamps burned.

As the days grew short, breakfast came before the working day began. There was, as always, barely time to swallow the meals, though the food was not as ample as it had been a year ago. At the end of the day now, she waited for Brigid, and they would go out together. Often all the other girls passed them on the stairs or in the yard, for they would be talking about what Brigid had read since the day before, and Lyddie would solve the mystery of an impossible word or the conundrum of a sentence.

Then one evening, she realized that Brigid was not beside her on the crowded stairs. She tried to wait, but the crowd of chattering operatives pushed her forward. She went down to the bottom of the stairs and stepped out of the stream. A hundred or more girls went past.

She was puzzled. Surely Brigid had been right beside her. They had been talking. Brigid had asked her what "thralldom" was. She was trying laboriously to read Mr. Douglass's book, but was yet to get through the first page of the preface.

At last the stairs were empty of clattering feet and the shrill laughter of young women at the end of a long workday. But still there was no Brigid. Lyddie hesitated. Perhaps the girl had gone ahead? Or perhaps she had forgotten something and gone back. Lyddie started across the nearly deserted yard. Her supper would be waiting and Mrs. Bedlow was insulted by tardiness. She had got nearly to the gate when something made her stop, nose up, like a doe with young in the thicket.

She hurried back and climbed the four flights to the weaving room. The lamps had been extinguished by the operatives as they left their looms, so at first her eyes could make out nothing but the hulking shapes of the machines.

Then she heard a strained, high-pitched voice. "Please, sir, please Mr. Marsden . . ."

Lyddie snatched up the fire bucket. It was full of water, but she didn't notice the weight. "Please—no—" She ran down the aisle between the looms toward the voice and saw in the shadows Brigid, eyes white with fear, and Mr. Marsden's back. His hands were clamped on Brigid's arms.

"Mr. Marsden!"

At the sound of her hoarse cry, the overseer whirled about. She crammed the fire bucket down over his shiny pate, his bulging eyes, his rosebud mouth fixed in a perfect little o. The stagnant water sloshed over his shoulders and ran down his trousers.

She let go of the bucket and grabbed Brigid's hand. They began to run, Lyddie dragging Brigid across the floor. Behind in the darkness, she thought she heard the noise of an angry bear crashing an oatmeal pot against the furniture.

She started to laugh. By the time they were at the bottom of the stairs she was weak with laughter and her side ached, but she kept running, through the empty yard, past the startled gatekeeper, across the bridge, and down the row of wide-eyed boardinghouses, dragging a bewildered Brigid behind her.

21

Turpitude

By morning the laughter was long past. She was awake and dressed, pacing the narrow corridor between the beds, before the four-thirty bell. Her breath caught high in her throat and her blood raced around her body, undecided whether to run fire through her veins, searing her despite the November chill, or freeze to the icy rivulet of a mountain brook.

She could not touch her breakfast. The smell of fried codfish turned her stomach. But she sat there amidst the chatter and clatter of the meal because it was easier to pass the time in the noise of company than in the raging silence of her room.

She was the first at the gate. It wasn't that she was eager for the day to begin, but eager for it to be over, for whatever was to happen—and she did not doubt that something dreadful must happen—for whatever must happen to be in the past.

She tried not to think of Brigid. She could not take on Brigid's fate as well as her own. If only she had not come back up the stairs. Monster! Would I have wished to leave that poor child alone? Better to feed Rachel and Agnes to the bear. And yet, Brigid was not a helpless child. She might have broken loose—stomped his foot or . . . Well, it was too late for that. Lyddie *had* gone back. She had, mercy on her, picked up that pail of filthy water and crammed it down on the overseer's neat little head. And all she had need to do was speak. When she had called his name, he had turned and let Brigid go. But, no, Lyddie could not be satisfied. She had taken that pail and rammed it till the man's shoulders were almost squeezed up under the tin. The skin on her scalp crawled . . .

Why didn't they open the gate? She was as weary of the scene in her head as if she'd actually picked up that heavy bucket and brought it down over and over again and run the length of the yard dragging Brigid behind her a thousand times over. Laughing. Of course he must have heard her. She had howled like a maniac. He must have heard.

The other operatives were crowded about, jostling her as they all waited for the bell. And still, when it rang, she jumped. It was so loud, so like an alarm clanging danger. She tried to turn against the tide, to get away while there was still time, but she was caught in the chattering, laughing trap of factory girls pushing themselves forward into the new day. She gave up and allowed the press of bodies around her to propel her to the enclosed staircase and up the four flights to the weaving room.

Brigid was not at her looms. Mr. Marsden was not on his high stool. Her execution was delayed. She felt relief, which was immediately swallowed up in anxiety. She needed it all to be over.

One of the girls from the Acre approached her. "Brigid says to tell you she's feeling a wee bit poorly this morning. You are not to worry."

The little coward. She's going to let me face it all alone, ey? When I was the one risked all to help her.

The girl glanced back over her shoulder and around the room. She bent her face close to Lyddie's neck and whispered. "The truth be told, she got word not to report this morning. But she had no wish to alarm you."

Now Lyddie was truly alarmed without even the slight armor that resentment might provide. Would they, then, be punishing Brigid instead of her? What sin had Brigid committed? What rule had she ever trespassed? And she with a sickly mother and nearly a dozen brothers and sisters to care for?

Mr. Marsden had come in. Lyddie kept her eyes carefully on her looms. The room shook and shuddered into life. Lyddie and the Irish girl beyond kept Brigid's looms going between them as best they could. She was almost busy enough to suppress her fears. And then a young man, the agent's clerk in his neat suit and cravat, appeared at her side and asked her to come with him to the agent's office. The time had come at last. She shut down her own looms and one of Brigid's, and followed the clerk down the stairs and out across the yard to the low building that housed the counting room and the offices.

The agent Graves was seated at his huge rolltop desk and did not at once turn from his papers and acknowledge her presence. The clerk had only taken her as far as the door, so she stood just inside as he closed it behind her. She tried to breathe.

She waited like that, hardly able to get a breath past her Adam's apple, until she began to feel quite faint. Would she collapse then in a heap on the rug? She studied the pattern, shades of dull browns, starting nearly black in the center and spinning out lighter and lighter to a dirty yellow at the outer edge. Dizzy, she stumbled a step forward to keep from falling. The man turned in his chair, as though annoyed. He was wearing half spectacles and he lowered his massive head and stared over them at her.

"You—you sent for me, sir?" It came out like a hen cackle. "Yes?"

"You sent for me, sir." She was glad to hear her voice grow stronger. The man kept staring as though she were a maggot on his dish. "Lydia Worthen, sir. You sent for me."

"Ah, yes, Miss Worthen." He neither stood nor asked her

to sit down. "Miss Worthen." He gathered the papers he had been working on and tamped the bottom of the pile on his desk to neaten it, and then laid the stack down on the right side of the desk. Then he scraped his chair around to face her more directly. "Miss Worthen. I've had a distressing interview with your overseer this morning."

She couldn't help but wonder how Mr. Marsden had retold last night's encounter.

"It seems," he continued, "it seems you are a troublemaker in the weaving room." He was studying her closely now, as closely as he had studied his papers before. "A troublemaker," he repeated.

"I, sir?"

"Yes. Mr. Marsden fears you are having a bad influence on the other girls there."

So there had been no report of last night. That, at least, seemed clear. "I do my work, sir," Lyddie said, gathering courage. "I have no intention of causing trouble on the floor."

"How long have you been with us, Miss Worthen?"

"A year, sir. Last April, sir."

"And how many looms are you tending at this time?"

"Four, sir."

"I see. And your wages? On the average?"

"I make a good wage, sir. Lately it's been three dollars above my board."

"Are you satisfied with these wages, then?"

"Yes, sir."

"I see. And the hours?"

"I'm used to long hours. I manage."

"I see. And none of this . . ." He waved a massive hand. "None of this ten-hour business, eh?"

"I never signed a petition." I meant to, but no need for you to know it.

There was a long pause during which the agent took off his

spectacles as though to see her better. "So," he said finally, "you are not one of these female reform girls?"

"No sir."

"I see," he said, replacing his spectacles and looking quite as though he saw much less than he had a few minutes before. "I see."

She took a tiny step forward. "May I ask, sir, why I'm being called a troublemaker?" She spoke very softly, but the agent heard her.

"Yes, well—"

"Maybe . . ." Her heart thumped in admiration for her own boldness. "Maybe Mr. Marsden could be called, sir? How is it, exactly, that I have displeased him?" Her voice went up to soften the request into a question.

"Yes, well . . ." He hesitated. "Open the door." And when Lyddie obeyed, he called to the clerk to summon Mr. Marsden, then turned again to Lyddie. "You may sit down, Miss Worthen," he said, and went back to the papers on his desk.

Though the chair he indicated was narrow and straight, she was grateful to sit down at last. The spurt of courage had exhausted her as much as her fear had earlier. She was glad, too, to have time to pull her rioting thoughts together. But the longer she waited, the greater the tumult inside her. So that when the clerk opened the door and Mr. Marsden appeared, she could only just keep from jumping up and crying out. She pressed her back into the spindles of the chair until she could almost feel the print of the wood through to her chest. She kept her eyes on the dizzying oval spiral of the rug.

There was a clearing of the throat and then, "You sent for me, sir?" Lyddie nearly laughed aloud. Her exact words, not ten minutes before.

The superintendent turned in his chair, but again he did not stand or offer the visitor a chair. "Miss Worthen here asks to know the charges against her."

Mr. Marsden coughed. Lyddie looked up despite herself. At her glance the overseer blinked quickly, then composed himself, his lids hooding his little dark eyes, his rosebud mouth tightening to a slit. "This one is a troublemaker," he said evenly.

She leapt to her feet. She couldn't seem to stop herself. "A troublemaker? Then what be you, Mr. Marsden? What be you, ey?"

The agent's head went up. His body was spread and his eyes bulged like a great toad, poised to spring. "Sit down, Miss Worthen!"

She sank onto the chair.

Her outburst had given the overseer the time he needed. He smiled slightly as though to say, See? No lady, this one.

Satisfied that he had stilled her, the agent shifted his gaze from Lyddie to her accuser. "A troublemaker, Mr. Marsden?" For a quick moment Lyddie hoped—but the man went on. "In what way a troublemaker? Her work record seems satisfactory."

"It is not"—and now Mr. Marsden turned and glared straight at Lyddie, all trace of nervousness gone—"it is not her work as such. Indeed," and here, he gave a sad little laugh, "I at one time thought of her as one of the best on the floor. But"—he turned back to the agent, his voice solemn and quiet—"I am forced, sir, to ask for her dismissal. It is a matter of moral turpitude."

Moral what? What was he saying? What was he accusing her of?

"I see," said the agent, as though all had been explained when nothing, nothing had.

"I cannot," and now the overseer's voice was fairly dripping with the honey of regret, "for the sake of all the innocent young women in my care, I cannot have among my girls someone who sets an example of moral turpitude."

"Certainly not, Mr. Marsden. The corporation cannot countenance moral turpitude."

She turned unbelieving from one man to the other, but they ignored her. She fought for words to counter the drift the interview had taken, but what could she say? She did not know what turpitude was. How could she deny something she did not even know existed? She knew what moral was. But that didn't help. Moral was Amelia's territory of faithful attendance at Sabbath worship and prayer meeting and Bible study, and she couldn't ask for consideration on those counts. She hardly ever went to worship, and Lord knew when she read, it wasn't just the Bible. Still, she was no worse than many, was she? At least she was not a papist, and no one was condemning them.

She opened her mouth. They were both looking at her sadly, but sternly. In the silence, the battle had been lost.

"You may ask the clerk for whatever wages are due you, Miss Worthen," the agent said, turning to his desk.

Mr. Marsden gave his superior's back a nod and tight rosebud smile. Did he click his heels? At any rate, he left quickly without another glance toward Lyddie.

"You may go now," the agent said without turning.

What could she do? She stumbled to her feet and out the door.

They paid her wages full and just, but there was no certificate of honorable discharge from the Concord Corporation, and with no certificate, she would never be hired by any other corporation in Lowell. She walked out of the tall gate benumbed. She had often dreamed of this last day, but in her dream she would be going home in triumph, and now there was no triumph and no home to go to even in disgrace.

22
Farewell

The bear had won. It had stolen her home, her family, her work, her good name. She had thought she was so strong, so tough, and she had just stood there like a day-old lamb and let it gobble her down. She looked around the crowded room that had been her home—the two double beds squeezed in with less than a foot between them for passage. She thought of Betsy sitting cross-legged on the one, bent slightly toward the candle, reading aloud while she, Lyddie, lay motionless, lost in Oliver's world.

And Amelia. Amelia would know what turp—turpitune, turpentine, whatever the wretched word was—Amelia was sure to know what it meant. She could see the older girl's eyebrows arch and her lips purse—"But *why* are you asking?" Indeed. So I can know what they charged against me—why I've lost my job, why I've been dismissed without a certificate. "You?" Betsy would laugh. "Not our Lyddie—Mr. Marsden's best girl." Meanwhile, Prudence would be busy explaining the meaning of the cussed word.

Thank God Rachel was safe. She had a home and food and school. She had a mother. And Charlie. I will not cry. She began to pack her things, stuffing them unfolded into the tiny gunnysack that had been her only luggage when she came. She almost laughed aloud. The sack wouldn't hold her extra clothes, much less her books. Well, she was a rich woman now. She could afford a proper trunk for her belongings even if she had no place to take them.

"They let me go," she explained to Mrs. Bedlow.

The landlady was incredulous. "But why?" she asked. "You were Mr. Marsden's best girl. Everyone said so."

Lyddie gave a laugh more like a horse whinny than any human sound. "Then everyone is wrong."

She could not bring herself to describe to Mrs. Bedlow the two encounters in the weaving room. She must, somehow, have caused the first. She knew so little of the ways of men and women that she must have, without realizing, given him some sign. Mr. Marsden was a deacon in his church. He was not a likable man, but surely . . . And last night. Mercy on her—she'd acted like a crazed beast. Why, even her own mother who died in an asylum had never gone wild like that.

She did not like Mr. Marsden. She had never liked him, but she had tried to please him—tried to win his approval by being the best. And though she needed to know what it was exactly that he was accusing her of, she knew he had not told the agent of those encounters. So, it was something else she had done wrong. She would have asked Mrs. Bedlow, but she was afraid the word would come out "turpentine" and Mrs. Bedlow would laugh. She couldn't bear to be laughed at, not just now.

"I'll be out of my room by tomorrow—the next day at the latest."

"But where will you go?" Don't worry for me. I can't stand it if you are kind, I might break down.

"Back to housekeeping, I reckon." That was it. Triphena would be sure to take her in.

She went to the bank and withdrew all her money—243 dollars and 87 pence. Then she went to the bookstore. She wanted to give Brigid a copy of *Oliver Twist* even if the girl couldn't really read it yet. She'd be able to in time.

"Will there be anything else for you today, Miss Worthen?" They were friends now, the bookseller and she. She hesitated, but what did it matter? She would never be in again. "Do you have a book that—that tells the meanings of words?"

"Ah," he said, "We have an old Alexander dictionary, of course, and then there's Webster's and Worcester's, which are more up-to-date."

"I think I need a up-to-date one," she said. She didn't want to risk buying one that didn't have the one word she needed.

The bookseller got down two fat books, Parts I and II of *An American Dictionary of the English Language* and then a third. "Many people prefer the Worcester," he said, indicating the third book. "It's a bit newer. And all in the one volume." Lyddie paid for the Worcester and forced herself to take it out of the shop before opening it.

As soon as she was out of sight of the bookshop window, she rested her parcels on the sidewalk and opened the dictionary. It took her some time to find the word. The pages were thin and her fingers calloused and clumsy, and she did not know the spelling. But she found it at last.

What? She would have howled in the street had it not been so crowded with passersby. She was not a vile or shameful character! She was not base or depraved. She was only ignorant, and what was the sin in that? He was the evil one to accuse her of such. She had done nothing evil, only foolish.

She rushed back to her room. What could she do? The damage was done. If only she had known what was going on when she was in the agent's office, how that vile man was lying. Oh, the agent was quick to believe him. When I cried out, it was I who was made to seem in the wrong! I was unladylike. That was my crime.

She wrote the letters in a fury, burning herself with sealing wax, her hand was shaking so. She rushed out of the house, her bonnet ribbons loose, her shawl flying. By the time she got to the Acre she was out of breath and could hardly ask the children playing in the streets where Brigid's house might be.

The first child she asked looked up with wide, frightened eyes and ran away without speaking. She stood long enough to tie her bonnet properly and catch her breath before asking another. He pointed dumbly to a shack that turned out not to be Brigid's house at all, but the housewife inside knew Brigid and gave Lyddie proper directions.

Brigid herself answered the door. "Oh Lyddie, what have they done?"

"I'm dismissed," Lyddie said.

"No, it cannot be."

"It can't be helped. It's done. But they must not dismiss you. I've already written a letter to Mr. Marsden. I told him if he dismissed you or bothered you in any way I would tell his wife exactly what happened in the weaving room. Now here is the letter addressed to her. If there is any problem you must mail it at once." Brigid stared at her, mouth open. "At once. You must swear to me you will." The girl nodded. "And now, I'd like to sit down if I could."

"Oh, I'm terrible rude." Brigid stepped aside and let her into the tiny shack. The smell was strong of food and body sweat. It was dark, but Lyddie could see children's eyes large and staring. "Me mother's housecleaning today." Brigid picked up a pile of what looked like rags, but might have been clothing, off a rough stool, and Lyddie sat down gratefully. She was still tired from last night. Tired as she had been after her sickness, her bones aching with it.

"Thank you," she said.

"Where will you be going? Not far from here, I hope."

"They didn't give me a certificate, so I have to go."

"And it's all me fault."

"No, you musn't blame yourself."

There was no place else to sit except the beds, so Brigid stood, watching her. In the darkness of the room, the only noise was the rustle of the children shifting, staring.

She had stopped gasping for breath. It was time to leave. "I'll be going, Brigid. Oh, yes. I nearly forgot." She handed the girl the parcel containing Brigid's old primer and *Oliver Twist.* "So you won't forget me altogether, ey?" she said, and fled so she wouldn't have to listen to Brigid's sobs.

That evening, just at the closing bell, she made her way down the street beyond the boardinghouse row to the trim, frame houses of the overseers of the Concord Corporation. She didn't know which house was his, but it didn't matter. He would have to come this way. She stood in the shadow of the first house and waited.

There was no mistaking his walk. Like a little bantam rooster, he came, all alone. Does he have any friends at all? She shoved the thought aside. She mustn't let anything dilute her anger. "Mr. Marsden?" She stepped out of the shadow and stood in his path.

He stopped, alarmed. They were nearly the same height and she stood close to his face and spoke with deadly quiet, the long brim of her bonnet nearly brushing his cheeks. "Yes, it's me, Lydia Worthen."

"Miss Worthen." He breathed out her name.

"I am mean and I am cheap. Sometimes I am a coward and often times I'm selfish. I ain't a beauty to look at. But I am not vile, shameful, base, or depraved!"

"Wha-at?"

"You accused me of moral turpitude, Mr. Marsden. I am here to say I am not guilty."

He stepped backward with a little puff of a gasp.

"I have here a letter I wrote. I will tell you what it says. It says if you cause Brigid MacBride to lose her position I will see that your wife is informed about what really happens in the weaving room after hours."

"My wife?" he whispered.

"Mrs. Overseer Marsden. I figure she ought to know if there is moral turpitude occurring in her husband's weaving room." She jammed the letter in the overseer's hand and closed his reluctant fist around it. "Good night, Mr. Marsden. I hope you sleep easy—before you die."

She took a stage to Boston. Hardly anyone did these days. The train was so much faster. But she had nowhere to go in such a hurry, and the ride gave her time to compose herself. Boston was a terrible place, older and even dirtier and more crowded than Lowell. The streets were narrow and Lyddie stepped gingerly around the refuse and animal droppings, lifting her skirt with one hand and trying to balance her new trunk under the other arm. She should have found a safe place to leave it, but how did one do that in an unknown city?

At last she found the address. She looked through a glass-windowed door and saw Diana herself, tall and pale, but no longer thin. She was speaking to a customer, her head slightly bent toward the short woman, a polite smile on her face.

Lyddie shifted the heavy trunk under her left arm and pushed open the door. A bell rang and Diana looked up at the sound. At first she nodded politely, her attention still with the chattering customer. Then she recognized Lyddie and her face was transformed.

"Excuse me a moment," she said to the woman, and came over and took the trunk. "Lyddie." Her voice was still quiet and beautifully low-pitched. "How wonderful to see you."

There was no time to talk until the customer's order was complete and the bell rang, signaling her departure. "How are you, Lyddie?" Diana asked.

"They dismissed me," she said. "For 'moral turpitude.' "

"For what?" Diana was almost laughing.

"It means—"

"I know what it means," Diana said gently. "I'm intimately acquainted with the term myself, but you . . . surely—"

"You are not vile, base, or depraved," Lyddie said.

"Thank you." Diana tried not to smile, but the corners of her mouth betrayed her. "And neither are you. What I can't imagine is how—"

"It was Mr. Marsden."

"Ah, yes, dear Mr. Marsden."

When Lyddie told the whole story, nearly crying again in her rage, she realized suddenly that Diana was shaking with laughter.

"It weren't funny, ey!" she protested.

"No, no, of course not. I'm sorry. But I'm imagining his face when you pounced out at him last night. Just when he thought he'd won—when he'd rid himself so neatly of the evidence."

Lyddie saw the rosebud mouth shaped into an **o** of fright. It *was* satisfying, wasn't it?

"And his wife is a perfect terror, but you know that—"

"I didn't think anyone else would believe me against him."

"Oh, she's a terror, all right. Everyone says so. She's a fright, I promise you." She got up and poured them each a cup of tea. "Let's celebrate, shall we? Oh Lyddie, it's so good of you to come. How can I help you?"

But she had come to help Diana. "I thought—I thought to help you if I could."

"Thank you, but I'm doing all right, as you can see. It was hard at first. No one seemed to want a husbandless woman expecting a child. But the proprietress here was ill and desperate for help. So we needed one another. It's worked out well. She's been so kind. And her daughter will look out for the baby when it comes." She smiled happily. "Like family to me." She reached over and patted Lyddie's knee. "But you understand."

Lyddie spent the night with Diana. Everyone was kind. Diana had her family at last. Then why had something snapped like a broken warp thread inside Lyddie's soul? Wasn't she happy for Diana? Surely, surely she was—happy and greatly relieved. "You must write to Brigid and tell her you are fine, ey?" Lyddie said as they parted the next morning. "She can read now, and she worries."

It rained all the way through New Hampshire, a steady, wearying drizzle. Lyddie rode inside the coach. There was only one other passenger, an old man who took no notice of her. She was grateful because she cried most of the way. She, tough-as-gristle Lyddie, her face in her handkerchief, her head turned toward the shaded window. But the tumult that had raged inside her damped down more and more as though beat into the muddy earth under the horses' hooves. When they finally crossed the bridge into Vermont, the sun came out and turned the leafless trees into silver against the deep green of the evergreen on the mountain slopes. The air was clean and cold, the sky blue, more like a bright day at winter's end than November.

23

Vermont,
November 1846

One more night along the way and the sky had turned into the underside of a thick quilt. The coachman pressed the team, eager to get to the next stop before the snow began to fall. It was nearly dusk when the coach took the final dash around the curve in the road that brought it to the door of Cutler's Tavern.

Nothing had changed except herself. At first Triphena pretended not to recognize her at all—"this grand lady come from the city of looms and spindles." But soon the game was over, and the old cook gave her a warm embrace and drew her to a seat by the giant fireplace.

"I would've thought you'd have a cook stove by now," Lyddie said half teasing, as she looked around the familiar kitchen.

"Not while I'm cook here," Triphena said fiercely. "I reckon everyone has those monstrosities in the city, ey?"

"They work fine. We had one at the boardinghouse."

Triphena sniffed. "They'll do, maybe, for those who ain't real cooks." She handed Lyddie a cup of her boiled coffee, thick with cream and maple sugar. "So you're for a visit home, ey?"

Lyddie was brought back with a pang to her present state. "I've left the factory," she said, "for good."

"So it's back to the farm, is it?"

"My uncle sold it."

"But what of your poor mother and the little ones?"

"Mama died," Lyddie said. There was no need to tell Triphena where. "And baby Agnes as well."

"Oh, dear," said Triphena softly.

"So Charlie took Rachel to live with him at the mill. The Phinneys have been good to them both. So—" She took a long drink from her coffee. It scalded her throat but she shook off the pain of it. "So—for the first time, I'm a free woman. Not a care—not a care in the world."

She paused, not knowing how to say, then, that she wished therefore to become once more a housemaid in Mistress Cutler's Tavern. "So—I thought to meself—what fun to work with Triphena again."

The cook threw her head back and laughed. *She thinks I'm joking. How to explain? How to say I've nowhere else to go?*

And then the girl came in. She was no more than twelve or thirteen, dressed in rough calico with ill-fitting boots. Lyddie's heart sank. *That was the housemaid.* There was no room for her at Cutler's Tavern anymore.

As it was, she spent the night in one of the guest rooms, paying full price, although Mistress Cutler pretended for a moment that she couldn't possibly take payment from an old and valued employee. Lyddie lay awake, wondering at the silence outside the window, the only light, the cloud-veiled moon. How could you sleep in such a quiet place with no rhythm and clatter from the street? Nothing at all to distract your head from wondering what on earth you could do, where you could go in a world that had no place for you, no need for you at all.

"Then you're off to see the children today?" said Triphena as she fed her breakfast at the great kitchen table. Lyddie was

178

grateful to have plans for at least one day. "The snow is no more'n a dusting. I can get Henry to take you in the wagon." Henry was Willie's successor.

Lyddie chose to walk. The day was cold and clear, but her shawl was warm and her boots stout and well broken in.

She was at the mill by mid-morning. Mrs. Phinney greeted her kindly, but Charlie and Rachel were gone to school in the village, so she just kept walking, her feet taking her up the hill road, past the fields and pastures of Quaker Stevens's farm, and on, up and beyond, until she rounded the last curve and saw it sitting there, squat and homely against the green and silver of the November mountain.

A tracery of snow lay on the fields and in the yard, but it was not true winter yet. In a week or so, everything would be sleeping under a thick comforter, but for now, the cabin stood out in all its sturdy homemade ugliness. Just like me, she thought, and blinked back tears. It was good to be home.

There was no wood piled against the door. Someone had stacked it neatly again in the woodshed. The door itself had been repaired and fit snugly now into its frame. She raised her father's wooden latch and pushed it open.

Even at the brightest midday, it was never really light inside the cabin. On a November afternoon it was truly dark. She found the flint box—no sulfur matches here—and lit the neatly laid tinder and logs. It was as though someone had prepared for her coming. She pulled her mother's rocker close and stared into the flames. Nothing smelled so good or danced so well as a birch fire. It was so full of cheer, so welcoming. Lyddie stretched her toes out toward the warmth of it and sighed, nearly content. She could almost forget everything. She was home where she had longed to be. Perhaps she could just stay the night here. No one would care. How could they deny her just one night before she left forever?

"Lyddie?"

She jumped up. There was the shape of a man, bent over low so as to clear the doorway. He stepped into the cabin and straightened tall. "Lyddie?" he said again, and she knew him for Luke Stevens. She was more angry at the interruption than ashamed to be caught.

"Lyddie?" he said a third time, "is it thee?" He took off his broad Quaker hat and held it over his stomach, squinting a little to see her through the darkness.

"I meant no harm," she said. "I just come to say good-bye." It sounded silly as she said it, coming to say good-bye to a cabin.

"Mother thought she saw thee pass. She sent me to fetch thee for supper and to stay the night if thee will."

She wished she could ask him just to let her stay here—for this one night. But there was no food, and she had no right to use up the Stevenses' kindling. She would not be beholden to them more than she could help. "I'll just be going back—"

"Please," he said, "stay with us. The dark comes so quick this time of year."

Her pride fought with her empty belly. But the truth was it had been hours since Triphena's breakfast, and the walk back would be long and dark and cold. "I've no wish to impose—"

"Thee must not think so," he said quickly. "It would pleasure our mother to have another woman in the house." He smiled shyly. "She often complains that none of us boys can seem to find a woman who will have us." He came to the fireplace and knelt to separate the logs and put out her small fire.

She was glad his back was to her and there was no chance that he could see her face flush red in the shadowy light of the cabin. "About your letter . . ." she began.

He shook his head without turning to her. "It was a foolish hope," he said quietly. "I pray thee forgive me."

They walked side by side down the road, the sun a blazing pumpkin as it fell rapidly behind the western mountains. Luke's long legs purposefully shortened their stride so that she would not have to skip to keep up. For a long time, neither spoke, but as the sun disappeared, and the dusk began to gather about them, he set his gaze far down the road ahead and asked softly, "Then if thee will not stay, where will thee go?"

"I'm off . . ." she said, and knew as she spoke what it was she was off to. To stare down the bear! The bear that she had thought all these years was outside herself, but now, truly, knew was in her own narrow spirit. She would stare down all the bears!

She stopped in the middle of the road, her whole body alight with the thrill of it. "I'm off," she said, "to Ohio. There is a college there that will take a woman just like a man." The plan grew as she spoke. "First I must go tomorrow to say good-bye to Charlie and little Rachel, and then I'll take the coach to Concord, and from there"—she took a deep breath—"the train. I'll go all the rest of the way by train."

He watched her face as though trying to read her thoughts, but gave up the attempt. "Thee is indeed a wonder, Lyddie Worthen," he said.

She looked up into his earnest face as he leaned to speak to her and saw in his bent shoulders the shade of an old man in a funny broad Quaker hat—the gentle old man that he would someday become and that she would love.

Tarnation, Lyddie Worthen! Ain't you learned nothing? Don't you know better than to tie yourself to some other living soul? You'd only be asking for trouble and grief. Might as well just throw open the cabin door full wide and invite that black bear right onto the hearth.

Still—if he was to wait—

He was looking right at her, his head cocked, his brown eyes questioning. His face was so close she could see a trace of soot on it. Like Charlie. The boy could never mess with a fire without getting all dirty. She held her hand tightly to her side to keep from reaching up and wiping his cheek with her fingers.

Will you wait, Luke Stevens? It'll be years before I come back to these mountains again. I won't come back weak and beaten down and because I have nowhere else to go. No, I will not be a slave, even to myself—

"Do I frighten thee?" he asked gently.

"Ey?"

"Thee was staring at me something fierce."

She began to giggle, as she used to when she and Charlie had been young.

His solemn face crinkled into lines of puzzlement and then, still not understanding, he crumpled into laughter, as though glad to be infected by her merriment. He took off his broad hat and ran his big hand through his rusty hair. "I will miss thee," he said.

We can stil hop, Luke Stevens, Lyddie said, but not aloud.

SPECIAL THANKS go to Mary E. Woodruff of the Vermont Women's History Project and Dr. Robert M. Brown of the Museum of American Textile History, who read this book in manuscript and offered suggestions and corrections. Any errors of fact which remain are, of course, my own.

I must also thank the library staff at the museum for their help and patience, Linda Willis at the Mid-State Regional Library of Vermont for locating and ordering materials for me, and Donald George of the Dairy Division of the Vermont State Agriculture Department for answering my questions about cows.

I cannot list all the books and publications to which I am indebted, but I must mention a few without which I could not have written this book:

Thomas Dublin's *Farm to Factory: Women's Letters, 1830–1860* and *Women At Work: The Transformation of Work and Community in Lowell, Massachusetts, 1826–1860*; Hannah Josephson's *The Golden Threads: New England's Mill Girls and Magnates*; David Macaulay's *Mill*; Abby Hemenway's nineteenth century compilation of stories from every section of Vermont, *Vermont Historical Gazetteer*, which includes a story of a hungry black bear that was the seed for the bear story in this book.

And the writings of the Lowell mill girls themselves, including Benita Eisler, editor, *The Lowell Offering: Writings by New England Mill Women (1840–45)*; Factory Tracts published by the Female Labor Reform Association as well as *Voice of Industry* issues from 1845–48; Lucy Larcom's *A New England Girlhood* and *An Idyl of Work*; and Harriet Hanson Robinson's *Loom and Spindle or Life Among the Early Mill Girls*.

About the Author

KATHERINE PATERSON's books have received wide acclaim and been published in eighteen languages. Among her many literary honors are two Newbery Medals and two National Book Awards. Her most recent book is *The Tale of the Mandarin Ducks*, illustrated by Leo and Diane Dillon. *Lyddie* came out of her participation in the Women's History Project celebrating Vermont's bicentennial in 1991.

The parents of four children, Mrs. Paterson and her husband live in Barre, Vermont.